KEEP OUT, CLAUDIA!

**Other books by
Ann M. Martin**

Rachel Parker, Kindergarten Show-off
Eleven Kids, One Summer
Ma and Pa Dracula
Yours Turly, Shirley
Ten Kids, No Pets
Slam Book
Just a Summer Romance
Missing Since Monday
With You and Without You
Me and Katie (the Pest)
Stage Fright
Inside Out
Bummer Summer

BABY-SITTERS LITTLE SISTER series
THE BABY-SITTERS CLUB mysteries
THE BABY-SITTERS CLUB series

KEEP OUT, CLAUDIA!

Ann M. Martin

AN
APPLE
PAPERBACK

SCHOLASTIC INC.
New York Toronto London Auckland Sydney

Cover art by Hodges Soileau

No part of this publication may be reproduced in whole or in part, or stored in a retrieval system, or transmitted in any form or by any means, electronic, mechanical, photocopying, recording, or otherwise, without written permission of the publisher. For information regarding permission, write to Scholastic Inc., 555 Broadway, New York, NY 10012.

ISBN 0-590-92582-2

12 11 10 9 8 7 6 5 4 3 2 1   10   6 7 8 9/9 0 1/0

Printed in the U.S.A.   40

For Olivia Ford
Thank you

KEEP OUT, CLAUDIA!

CHAPTER 1

"Claudia? Do you think Shea is playing that song right?" Jackie Rodowsky wanted to know. He gazed at me from under a fringe of red bangs.

I listened carefully to the piano music drifting from the living room. "What's he supposed to be playing?" I asked.

Jackie shrugged. " 'A doggie-o.' "

" 'A doggie-o'?" I repeated. I had never heard of "a doggie-o." Then again, I don't know much about music, except that I like certain groups and singers. And that I have recently started to like Bach. No kidding. His music is awesome, if you really listen to it.

From the other room I heard plink, plinkety, plink, plink, *blam*. (Oops.) Shea started over. Plink, plinkety, plink, plink, *blam*.

"Bullfrogs!" Shea yelled.

"I guess he isn't playing it right," said Jackie.

"I guess not."

"Duh," added Archie, who is Jackie and Shea's little brother.

It was Monday afternoon and I was baby-sitting at the Rodowskys' for three freckle-faced redheads. Shea is nine, Jackie is seven, and Archie is four. Shea was practicing for his upcoming piano recital. I hoped he would be ready.

Blam. "Bullfrogs!"

Jackie and Archie giggled.

Then Jackie looked up from the enormous rocket ship he and Archie were building with Legos. The Rodowsky boys have a Lego supply bigger than what you could find in most toy stores. "I wish I could play the piano. Or some instrument," Jackie said. He reached for a handful of Legos — and knocked a fin off the spaceship. The fin fell to the floor and split into pieces just as Bo, the Rodowskys' dog, tore into the rec room. He skittered on the Legos and crashed into the table on which the spaceship was being built.

"Cowabunga!" shrieked Archie, as the table collapsed and the rocket ship slid to the floor and smashed.

Jackie looked at me balefully. "Was that my fault?" he asked.

I tried to smile. "Not really," I told him. "Bo helped. Maybe Bo needs some exercise. Why don't you take him outside? Archie and I will try to put the spaceship back together."

Jackie sighed. "Okay," he replied. "But don't be surprised if I ram into the toolshed or wreck up the lawn or something."

Jackie is the teeniest bit accident-prone. Sometimes this bothers him — but mostly he is pretty happy-go-lucky.

Plink, plinkety, plink, plink, *blam*. "Bullfrogs!"

"You know what *I* wish, Claudia?" Archie said when Jackie and Bo were safely out the door. "I wish I could be in a play. Or in a show. I want to stand on a stage in front of a lot of people. I want the people to clap for me, and laugh at my jokes."

"You want to be an entertainer?" I said. "Hmm. And Jackie wants to play an instrument, and Shea is getting ready for his recital. You guys must like show business."

"Yup," replied Shea. "Don't you?"

To be truthful, I hadn't given it much thought. I have other interests. Like art and baby-sitting. And junk food.

My name is Claudia Kishi. Claudia Lynn Kishi, to be exact. I'm thirteen years old. I live here in the small town of Stoneybrook, Connecticut. I have a mom and a dad and an older sister. I don't have any pets, but I do have lots of friends. My best friends are the members of a business called the Baby-sitters Club. I happen to be the vice-president of that club (which us members call the BSC).

I've been the vice-president of the BSC ever since the club started, which was back at the beginning of seventh grade. Now I'm in eighth grade at Stoneybrook Middle School. I'll tell you a secret about school and me. I am not a very good student. I am especially not a good speller. It isn't that I'm dumb, although sometimes I *feel* dumb. It's just that I don't think school is very interesting. Except for art class. And when I'm at home I can usually find about a dozen things to do that are more exciting than homework. My parents say I have to learn discipline and responsibility. I say I am disciplined and responsible . . . but who needs to know about hypotenuses (hypotenusi?) or what letter "psychiatrist" begins with? (Anyone with half a brain would spell that word "sikiatrist." It would make much more sense. Furthermore, if you really think about it, in general, you hardly need the letter "c" at all. You could spell most "c" things with an "s" or a "k." You only need that "c" for spelling "chocolate" or "cheesecake," which by the way, *could* be spelled "choklit" and "chezkak." Just a thought. But is it any wonder I'm a bad speller?)

I'll tell you something. I bet I wouldn't feel

dumb sometimes if my sister Janine wasn't so smart. Janine is a genius. She is sixteen and basically a junior at Stoneybrook High, but already she takes courses at the local college. She did that last year, too. Can you imagine? She was fifteen and going to school with students who were, like, six years older than she was. Well, some of them were. And Janine's grades were as good as theirs. Or better. I think I'm just dumb by comparison. What I mean is I'm *not* dumb. But next to Janine I *look* dumb.

Maybe if I got glasses and dressed in frumpy, dowdy clothes like Janine — no. I could never do that. I hope this doesn't sound conceited or shallow, but clothes and fashion are very important to me. Well, they are. They're almost as important as art and children and baby-sitting. I like to look good, and I'm good at looking good. All my friends say so. Sometimes they even copy my style. I wear pretty trendy clothes, and I like to be imaginative and try new things. I have to admit that the money I earn baby-sitting goes for art supplies (first) and then for jewelry and accessories and stuff. I have not saved much at all. (Unlike my friends Kristy and Jessi who hoard their money like squirrels hoard acorns.)

As Archie and I knelt on the floor and picked up pieces of the rocket ship, I thought about the upcoming meeting of the BSC. My friends and I hold our meetings in my bedroom, and we were due for one later that afternoon. Mrs. Rodowsky had said she would be home before five, and the meeting would begin at five-thirty. Perfect. That would give me just enough time to fly home and straighten up my room. Ordinarily I don't bother. (My friends are used to my messes.) But that day my room was extra messy because I'd been experimenting with making ceramic mobiles, and little figures and pieces of wire were *every-where*. (Along with Snickers bars and M&M's and Neccos and Fritos and ranch-style potato chips and crackers and popcorn . . .)

The back door opened and Bo bounded into the room, followed by Jackie. "The toolshed is still standing," Jackie announced. "If I broke anything out there, I don't know about it."

I smiled. "Don't worry. You didn't mean to bump into the rocket ship. It was just an accident."

"An*oth*er accident," Jackie corrected me.

"Well, anyway, Archie and I have already put most of the spaceship back together. See? It broke into big pieces."

Jackie the walking disaster grinned. "Good," he said.

Plink, plinkety, plink, plink, *blam*. "Bullfrogs!" yelled Shea. (This time even *he* giggled.)

"Hey, Shea! You can stop practicing now!" I called. "Time's up."

"Okay!" he called back. But he didn't stop. I think he was getting worried about the recital.

"Lucky-duck Shea," said Archie as we lifted the spaceship back onto the table. "I could put on a show, too, you know. I can play 'Mary Had a Little Lamb' on the piano."

"With one finger," murmured Jackie. Then he hurried on. "I bet I could play the . . . the, um, the . . . well, I could play something."

"And I could dance," added Archie, "and sing. I could be a star."

Mrs. Rodowsky came back promptly at 4:45 that afternoon. As soon as she had paid me, I climbed onto my bicycle and pedaled home. As I rode along, I thought about Jackie, who wished he could play an instrument, and about Archie's words: "I could be a star." It was time for my friends and me to cook up a musical project for the kids we sit for. Obviously the Rodowsky boys would want to be involved in something like that. And I was sure other kids would, too.

I was so lost in thought when I reached

home that I nearly tripped over Janine who was sitting on our front stoop reading one of her sociology texts. Her bookbag was perched beside her.

"Oof! Sorry," I said. "What are you doing here?" The weather that day was gorgeous — warm and sunny — but Janine prefers to study in her room. She is not an outdoor person.

"I'm locked out," she said. "I can't find my key."

"Well, I'm here to save the day," I replied.

Our parents both work, so at my house forgetting or losing your key could mean trouble. Dad is a broker with a company in Stamford, Connecticut, which is the nearest city, and Mom is the head librarian at the Stoneybrook Public Library.

I unlocked the front door and let Janine inside.

She checked her watch. "You have a meeting soon, don't you?"

"Yup," I said. "I'm going to clean up my room. Want to keep me company?" Janine may be dowdy, and she may be a genius who makes me look dumb next to her, but she is still my sister, and I love her.

"All right." Janine followed me upstairs and along the hall to my room. "Goodness. What are you working on?" she asked. She cleared a space on my bed so she could sit down.

"Mobiles," I answered. "Want to see?" I held up a half-finished one with ceramic cowboy boots, a cactus, and a coyote hanging from delicate curving wires. Then I showed her a still life I was painting, a charcoal sketch I was finishing up, and an idea for making jewelry with beads, sequins, and lace. And then I began to tidy up.

Janine watched with a half smile as I dug a package of Ring-Dings out from under a pile of papers and drawings on my desk, and tried to make order out of chaos. "Are you going to be ready in time?" she asked.

"Barely," I answered.

And at that moment I heard our front door open and close, and then feet running up the stairs. "I'm here!" yelled Stacey McGill.

CHAPTER 2

By five-thirty, Janine had left my room and settled herself in front of her computer. In her place were the six other members of the Babysitters Club: Kristy Thomas, Mary Anne Spier, Stacey McGill, Dawn Schafer, Jessi Ramsey, and Mallory Pike.

"This meeting of the BSC will now come to order," announced Kristy. She was sitting in my director's chair, one leg crossed over the other, a visor perched on her head, a pencil stuck over her ear, and a notebook open in her lap. Kristy is the president. She gets to call meetings to order. (She has a mouth which is suited to that purpose.)

It seems like forever that my friends and I have met in my room every Monday, Wednesday, and Friday afternoon from five-thirty until six but, as I mentioned, the BSC has only been around since the beginning of seventh grade. The club was Kristy's idea, and when it first began, there were just four members — Kristy, Stacey, Mary Anne, and me. As business grew, so did the club. Soon Dawn joined, and later Mal and Jessi joined, too.

How does our business work? It's simple, really. When parents in Stoneybrook (especially in our neighborhood) need a sitter for their children, they call us during one of our club meetings. Since they reach seven capable sitters at once, they're bound to line up someone with just one call (instead of making a million phone calls, trying to find a sitter who's free). My friends and I get tons of jobs this way, which is great, since we *adore* children. (We like the money we earn, too.)

As president, Kristy runs things smoothly and professionally. Every club member has her own duties and responsibilities. Kristy's duties are to be in charge, and to keep coming up with her good ideas. Kristy is famous for her ideas. She thought up the club, and she thought up a lot of other things. Like Kid-Kits. A Kid-Kit is a cardboard box (we each have one now) that we've decorated and filled with our old books, toys, and games, plus art supplies, activity books, and so on. We often take them along when we go on a sitting job. Kids love to explore them, which is one reason we're popular sitters.

Kristy also decided that keeping a notebook

and a record book would help our club to be efficient and organized. The notebook is more like a diary. In it, each of us writes up every single job we go on. Then we're responsible for reading the notebook once a week to find out how our friends solved sitting problems, and to stay in touch with the lives of our clients. The record book is where we keep track of all kinds of information: our clients' names, addresses, and phone numbers; the rates they pay; and notes about the children we sit for regularly, such as whether they have food allergies or special fears, or have to take any kind of medication. These things are extremely helpful to us.

Sometimes when I think about all the great ideas Kristy has had for the BSC, I'm amazed. At other times I think that's just part of who Kristy is. She's always had great ideas. I should know since she and Mary Anne and I grew up together. Before our lives began to change, our families lived on Bradford Court. Kristy lived across the street from me, and Mary Anne lived next door to her. (Now I'm the only one who still lives on Bradford Court.) Anyway, even when we were little kids Kristy had one great idea after another. Who knows why?

Kristy's family is a pretty interesting one, as far as I'm concerned. She has two older brothers, Sam and Charlie (they're in high school with my sister), and a little brother David Michael (he's seven). Her dad walked out on the family when David Michael was just a baby. For a long time, Kristy's mother struggled to support her four kids by herself — and she did a terrific job. She's some kind of big executive with a company in Stamford. When Kristy was in seventh grade her mom met and fell in love with a man named Watson Brewer. Guess what. Watson is an actual millionaire. And during the summer between seventh and eighth grade, Watson and Kristy's mom got married, and Watson moved the Thomases into his mansion (yes, mansion) across town. So Kristy acquired a stepfather. At the same time she acquired a little stepsister and stepbrother, Karen and Andrew, who are seven and four. Later, she acquired an adopted sister! Not long ago, Watson and Kristy's mom adopted Emily Michelle, a two-and-a-half-year-old girl who had been born in Vietnam.

As you can imagine, the Thomas/Brewer household is pretty wild sometimes. Even though Karen and Andrew live there only part time (mostly, they live with their mother and stepfather, who are also in Stoneybrook), the house is zooey, what with all those kids, Kristy's grandmother Nannie (who moved in to help care for Emily), and various pets.

What sort of person is Kristy? Well, she's energetic and outgoing and she talks a lot. Even *she* admits she has a big mouth. She loves sports and kids, which is why she decided to organize and coach a softball team for little kids, called Kristy's Krushers. Kristy has a fun sense of humor, and she's a good student. She's brown-eyed and brown-haired and the shortest kid in her class. (By the way, Kristy is thirteen, like me. So are the other members of the Baby-sitters Club, except for Mal and Jessi who are eleven and in sixth grade.) One thing that does *not* interest Kristy is clothes. She's happiest wearing jeans and a sweat shirt, maybe a turtleneck, baggy socks, old running shoes, and sometimes a baseball cap. If forced, she will put on a little makeup or jewelry, but she rarely thinks of that herself.

Would you be surprised to find out that Kristy has a boyfriend? Well, she does, although I think she'd kill me if she heard me say that. But she and Bart Taylor, who lives in her new neighborhood, have been spending a lot of time together, and not just on the softball field (Bart coaches a rival team, Bart's Bashers). They've even gone to a few school dances together.

Let's see. On to the vice-president of the BSC, and that's me. You already know a lot about me and my family, but let me tell you why I was elected V.P. It is mainly because I have a phone in my room. Not only that, I have my very own phone *number*. This is important, considering how many calls we usually receive during a club meeting. Using a parent's phone would be pretty inconvenient (we'd tie it up three times a week and get calls during meetings that were for other people). So we're lucky to have my phone. As vice-president, I also offer around my supply of junk food when my friends and I meet. More importantly, I deal with calls that come in when we're not meeting.

One last thing about me. I'm Japanese-American. This is what I look like: extra-long black hair, almond-shaped eyes, and a good complexion, especially considering the amount of junk food I eat.

Mary Anne Spier is the secretary of the club. Her duties are complicated — to schedule each and every job that is phoned in. To do that, she has to know when I have art lessons, when Mal has orthodontist appointments, when Jessi will be at her ballet classes, and so forth. She keeps track of our jobs on the appointment pages in the record book. As far as anyone knows, she has never made a mistake. Mary Anne is also in charge of keeping the entire record book up-to-date and in order.

When I tell you about the kind of person

Mary Anne is, I think you'll be surprised to find out that she's Kristy's best friend. I'm still surprised — and I've known Mary Anne and Kristy all my life. Okay, remember that Kristy has a big mouth? Well, Mary Anne is quiet and softspoken, shy and sentimental. She cries easily. She is *so* sensitive. Not that Kristy is *in*sensitive; but she's tough-skinned, and Mary Anne is not. Still, Mary Anne is a survivor. Her life hasn't been exactly easy. Her mom died when Mary Anne was little and, after that, Mary Anne was raised by her *very* strict father. Mr. Spier loves his daughter, that's for sure, but he overprotected her and treated her like a baby. Only recently was Mary Anne allowed to wear her hair long (instead of in braids) and to choose her own clothes (which are slowly becoming trendier and less little-girl-like). It's practically a miracle that she has a steady boyfriend, Logan Bruno. But she does. They've been going out for quite awhile now (except for the time when they were going through The Big Separation). Logan is a really great guy. He's sweet, and he's very understanding of Mary Anne. He's also an associate member of the BSC. Honest. He's a terrific baby-sitter, so we call on him at those times when a job comes in that the rest of us can't take. (Or we call on Shannon Kilbourne.

She's our other associate member; she lives across the street from Kristy.)

You will never guess what happened to Mary Anne Spier earlier this year. Her dad finally remarried, so Mary Anne wound up with a stepmother, a stepbrother, and a stepsister. Here's the unbelievable part. Her stepsister is Dawn Schafer, Mary Anne's other best friend. Can you imagine having a best friend who becomes your stepsister?

This is the story. In the middle of seventh grade, Dawn moved to Stoneybrook with her mother and her brother Jeff after her parents got divorced. They moved clear across the country from California, where Dawn and Jeff had been born, since their *mother* had been born here in Stoneybrook. Dawn and Mary Anne became friends right away, and soon Dawn joined the Baby-sitters Club. Around the same time Mr. Spier began going out with Mrs. Schafer and poof! They got married. The next thing we knew, Mary Anne, her dad, and her kitten Tigger had moved into Dawn's house (it's bigger than the one Mary Anne had lived in), and Mary Anne and Dawn had become stepsisters. Whew. You never know what's around the corner.

Here's a theory of mine: Life is just one big surprise.

I guess I should tell you about Dawn next since I've sort of introduced you to her already. Our California girl is the alternate officer of the BSC. If anyone can't make a club meeting, Dawn steps in and takes over her duties. This means she has to know how to do everyone's jobs, which isn't easy. But Dawn is dependable. We can always count on her.

Dawn is also an individual. She tends to go her own way, and not worry much about what other people think. I don't mean she's uncaring. I just mean that she believes what she wants to believe, does the things she wants to do, dresses the way she wants to dress, and so on without being swayed by other people's opinions. If kids don't agree with Dawn, she doesn't care (much). She's a very strong person. I really admire her.

Dawn has lo-o-o-o-ong blonde hair. It's about the color of corn silk. Her eyes are blue. When she lived in California she sported a nice tan, but that has faded, thanks to our Connecticut winters. Remember I said that I'm a junk-food addict? Well, Dawn is a health-food addict. She lives on fruits, vegetables, and stuff like tofu and rice. No red meat or sugar for her. I could live without meat, I think, but it's the sugar thing I don't understand. How does Dawn live without Twinkies and Three Musketeers bars?

Okay, it's time for me to tell you about *my* best friend. She's Stacey McGill, the treasurer of the BSC. Stacey (who's an only child) lives in Stoneybrook (duh), but she's a New York City girl at heart. That's where she grew up. And her dad still lives there. Like Dawn, Stacey and her mom settled here after the McGills got a divorce. But Stace is much more like me than like Dawn. We're sophisticated and boy-crazy, although we don't have steady boy-friends. And we love fashion. Stacey is allowed to wear pretty much whatever she wants, and to have her blonde hair permed. *Un*like me, Stacey is excellent at math, which is how she became the club treasurer. Stacey's in charge of keeping track of the money we earn, and of collecting our dues every Monday. Then she doles out the dues money as it's needed — to help pay my phone bills, to buy new items for the Kid-Kits, and so forth.

Also, unlike me, Stacey can't eat sweets. This is because she has a disease called diabetes. Her body doesn't process sugar the way it should, so Stacey has to help things along by sticking to a strict diet, and giving herself injections (yes, in*jec*tions) of something called insulin. None of this is easy, but Stacey copes well. I guess she's a survivor, too. (Actually, in our own way, we're all survivors.)

The two youngest officers of the Baby-sitters Club are our junior members, Jessi and Mal. "Junior member" means that they are too young to be allowed to sit at night, unless they're sitting for their own brothers and sisters and, believe me, they have plenty of brothers and sisters between them. Jessi has one younger sister and a baby brother, and Mal has *seven* brothers and sisters. She's the oldest of eight kids.

Jessi and Mal are another pair of best friends. And Jessi is another newcomer to Stoneybrook. Her family moved here at the beginning of the school year when her father's job changed. (Mal grew up in Stoneybrook.) Jessi is an extremely talented ballet dancer, and Mal likes to write and draw, and plans to create picture books when she's older.

Jessi and Mal don't look a thing alike. Jessi is African-American. Her skin is the color of cocoa, and (because of her dance classes) she often wears her hair up, or pulled back. Her legs are the long legs of a dancer and her eyelashes are so long she looks as if she's wearing mascara, even though she isn't allowed to use makeup.

Mal is white. Her hair is red and curly, and her face is covered with freckles. Plus, she wears glasses and braces. Her braces are the clear kind that don't show up much. Even so, Mallory doesn't feel particularly attractive. At least she and Jessi were allowed to have their ears pierced. Now if Mal could just get contact lenses, but her parents say no; not until she's older.

I have a feeling that both Jessi and Mal spend quite a bit of time wishing they were older. They think eleven is the pits. They feel grown-up and want to be treated as adults, but their parents still see them as kids, even when they baby-sit. Oh, well. Everyone is eleven at one time. We all live through it.

"Thank you . . . thank you . . . thank you . . ." The Monday afternoon meeting of the BSC was underway, and Stacey was collecting our dues. She was being very polite, considering none of us particularly likes to part with our money.

When she had finished, and had added our dues to the treasury (a manila envelope), the room grew quiet. We were waiting for the phone to ring. When it didn't, I decided to tell my friends about my afternoon with the Rodowsky boys.

"And so," I said finally, "what I've been thinking is that maybe we should come up with some kind of project — planning a musical performance — with the kids we sit for. Whoever's interested."

"That's a terrific idea!" exclaimed Jessi.

"But what, exactly, should we do?" I asked. "I mean, we've helped the kids put on some plays and skits already."

"And none of *us* is terribly musical," Kristy pointed out.

"I don't think that matters too much," said Mal. "We can help the kids organize and plan a show or something. They'll learn a lot just by experimenting. And don't forget. Some of *them* are pretty musical."

"Like the Perkins girls," I said.

"And Shea Rodowsky," added Mary Anne. "Remember his piano lessons. Other kids take lessons, too, like Marilyn Arnold. Plus, we can help them play simple homemade instruments such as drums — you know, oatmeal cartons? — and bells and tambourines."

Ring, ring.

"And telephones," said Stacey, giggling. Then she composed herself and reached for the receiver. "Hello, Baby-sitters Club," she said. A pause followed. Then, "Yes? . . . Yes. . . . Oh, mm-hmm." She was not talking to one of our regular clients. It was somebody she didn't know well. Stacey jotted down a few notes and told the caller she'd phone back in a few minutes. When she hung up, she was smiling. "New clients," she announced. "They saw one of our fliers."

"Cool," said Dawn. "Who are they?"

"Their name is Lowell. That was Mrs. Lowell. She and her husband have three children. They're eight, six, and three. Two girls and a boy, I think she said. She doesn't know much about us. Just what she read in the flier. Also, she heard from somewhere that we're very reliable."

"Our reputation is spreading," said Kristy proudly.

"She needs a sitter for Friday afternoon," Stacey continued. She glanced at Mary Anne who was already checking the record book.

"Let's see. Mal, you're free." Mary Anne frowned. "And Claud, so are you, unless you're going to that art thing you mentioned last week. Oh, and I'm free. Who wants the job?"

"I told Vanessa I'd take her to the bookstore on Friday," said Mal. (Vanessa is Mallory's nine-year-old sister. She's a bookworm, like Mal.)

"And I did decide to go to the 'art thing,' " I said. "It's an art *show*. At a gallery."

"That leaves me." Mary Anne penciled herself in for the job. Then Stacey telephoned Mrs. Lowell to tell her who to expect on Friday.

The numbers on my digital clock flipped from 5:59 to 6:00.

"Well, I guess that's that," said Kristy. "Good meeting, you guys."

My friends and I stood up. Kristy removed the pencil from over her ear and stuck it in the back pocket of her jeans.

"See you in school tomorrow!" Jessi called to Mal as they ran down the hallway to the staircase.

"I'll call you tonight!" Mary Anne said to Kristy.

"Kristy, your brother's here to pick you up!" Dawn yelled.

And Stacey, my best friend, said, " 'Bye, Claud. Phone me tonight and we'll *tawk*." I laughed. I watched my friends leave the house.

CHAPTER 3

Friday

Today I met the Lowell
kids. They are Caitlin (eight),
Mackenzie (six), and Celeste
(three). Mackenzie is called
Mackie. I love those names!
Caitlin, Mackie, and Celeste.
And I love the kids. They're
really pretty, all three of
them. They look kind of like
china dolls. Uh-oh. I'm off
the subject.

When I arrived at the
Lowells' house, Mrs. Lowell
was waiting to show me
around. She's very organized.
And the kids seemed obedient
and helpful.

25

Mary Anne's afternoon with the Lowell kids was easy, especially considering it was a new job. Sometimes an unfamiliar baby-sitter can be upsetting to kids, but the Lowells were as good as gold, according to Mary Anne.

Promptly at three-thirty, Mary Anne rang the Lowells' bell. Mrs. Lowell answered the door. Before she said hello, she glanced up and down at Mary Anne. She did it very quickly, but Mary Anne said it made her feel kind of strange, like she was being inspected. Anyway, Mrs. Lowell must have approved of what she saw because she stretched her mouth into a smile. Then she said, "I guess you're Mary Anne Spier." She seemed like any other mom.

"Yes," Mary Anne replied. And then she added formally, "From the Baby-sitters Club." She held up her Kid-Kit as if it were proof of this.

"Come inside. I'm Denise Lowell. I'm glad you were available. Do you mind if I ask you some questions?"

Mary Anne shook her head. "Nope."

"Terrific." Mrs. Lowell and Mary Anne sat in the kitchen. "So you are . . . how old?" asked Mrs. Lowell.

"Thirteen."

"And how long have you been baby-sitting?"

"About two years. Before that, some moms let me be mother's helpers, though. I've taken care of all ages of kids, even babies."

Mrs. Lowell nodded with satisfaction. Then she told Mary Anne where to find emergency numbers. And *then* she called, "Children! Caitlin, Mackie, Celeste!"

In less than a minute, the Lowell kids had run into the kitchen and were standing in a line. At first, Mary Anne just gazed at them. This was when she decided they looked like dolls. The children stood silently in their line. They didn't smile, but they gazed back at Mary Anne with clear blue eyes. The children were blond, their hair as light as Dawn's, and their complexions were pale. Caitlin and Mackie were dressed in what Mary Anne guessed were private school uniforms. Caitlin wore a blue plaid skirt, a blazer, a white blouse and white tights, and red shoes. Mackie wore neatly pressed pants, a blazer, and brown oxfords. And Celeste, a large bow in her hair, was wearing a white blouse and a pink pinafore.

"Thank you, children," said their mother after a moment, and the kids left the kitchen quietly. Mrs. Lowell turned to Mary Anne.

"I'll only be gone for about an hour and a half today," she said, and gave Mary Anne a short list of instructions. A few moments later, she left. Celeste cried briefly, then calmed down.

"So what do you guys want to do this afternoon?" asked Mary Anne. She was in the family room, holding the sniffling Celeste in her lap.

Caitlin looked thoughtful. "Tell us about your family," she said.

Mary Anne was startled. "My family?"

"Yeah. Do you have any pets?"

"Oh." Mary Anne smiled. She likes curious kids. "I have a kitten," she replied. "His name is Tigger."

"What color is he?" asked Mackie.

"And is he a he or a she?" asked Caitlin.

"He's a he. And he's gray striped."

"Does he talk?" Celeste tipped her head back to see Mary Anne's face. Her tears were drying on her cheeks.

"Does he talk? Well, he mews," said Mary Anne.

"Do you pre*tend* he talks?" Celeste pressed.

"Sometimes."

"Do you have brothers and sisters?" asked Caitlin. Then she added, "I'm lucky. I have one of each."

"Me, too," said Mary Anne. "Well, really they are my stepbrother and stepsister. Guess what. My stepsister is also my best friend. And she's the same age as me."

"Ooh," said Mackie. "What's a stepsister?"

Mary Anne tried to explain. When she had finished, she said, "Dawn is also a baby-sitter, like me. We both belong to the Baby-sitters Club."

Well, of course then Caitlin wanted to know about the other members of the BSC. Mary Anne began with Mallory. "She has *seven* brothers and sisters!" she exclaimed.

Caitlin raised her eyebrows. "She must be Catholic," she said.

Mary Anne raised her own eyebrows. "I — " she began to say.

But Mackie interrupted her. "What religion are you?" he asked.

"Well . . . my family doesn't go to church very often," Mary Anne replied, "but when we do, we go to the Presbyterian Church."

"Tell us more about your kitty," said Celeste. By that time she had turned herself around so that she was sitting face to face with Mary Anne. "Do you dress him up?"

So many questions! Mary Anne had never encountered kids like the Lowells. Even Karen Brewer (Kristy's little sister) who is an incredible talker, doesn't ask question after question. (Maybe that's because she'd rather talk than listen.)

Mary Anne told Celeste that Tigger doesn't like to wear clothes (he prefers his fur), and then she managed to engage the kids in some outdoor games, after they had changed their clothes of course. They played mother, may I? and red light, green light, statues, and hide-and-seek.

Finally, Celeste plopped herself down on the lawn and said, "I'm tired. My legs won't hold me up anymore."

"Let's go inside then," said Mary Anne. "Caitlin? Do you have homework?"

"Not on Friday!"

"How about you, Mackie?"

"Not in first grade!"

"Can we watch TV?" asked Caitlin. "*Leave It to Beaver* is on. Mommy always lets us watch that."

"Sure," replied Mary Anne, and she led the kids inside. They settled themselves in the family room — but no one could find *Leave It to Beaver*, no matter how often Caitlin switched the channels.

Soon Celeste grew bored, so Mary Anne found crayons and paper. Celeste announced that she was going to draw a picture of Tigger.

"Great," replied Mary Anne. "I'll watch."

It was while Celeste was adding huge purple eyes to Tigger's wobbly, wavy head that Mary Anne heard giggling from Caitlin and Mackie.

"Did you find *Leave It to Beaver*?" she asked. She glanced at the TV, but saw only an Asian girl and boy riding their bicycles along a neighborhood street.

The show was in color, so Mary Anne knew it wasn't *Leave It to Beaver*. Also, she guessed she had missed the funny part. Then she heard Mackie cry, "Look at their eyes!" and giggle harder.

Mary Anne glanced at the TV again. The scene hadn't changed. She shrugged, not seeing the humor. Oh, well.

"Hello!" called a voice as the back door opened and closed.

"Mommy!" shrieked Celeste, and abandoned her drawing. She raced to her mother and wrapped her arms around Mrs. Lowell's knees.

Five minutes later, Mary Anne was dashing across the Lowells' yard on her way to my house for Friday's meeting of the BSC. She arrived breathless. And early.

So did Kristy. The three of us piled onto my bed for a chat, just like we used to do years ago when we were little.

"Hey, guess what," I exclaimed. "I had a great idea!"

"That's *my* job," teased Kristy.

"No, really. I was thinking about Jackie and his brothers and a musical performance or something, and well, how about helping the kids form a band? The kids who take music lessons can play their own instruments and the other kids can *make* instruments, like you suggested Mary Anne."

"Way cool!" said Kristy. And she wasn't the only one who felt that way. After the meeting started, Kristy asked me to tell the others about the band. Everyone liked the idea.

"Excellent," said Kristy. "There's nothing like a new project."

CHAPTER 4

"Round and round and round she goes," I said, circling my finger in the air, "where she'll stop, nobody . . . knows!" When I said *knows* I touched the nose of Lucy Newton, who squealed with laughter.

Lucy is just a baby, and she loves that game. But Jamie, her brother, is four and wants to do more grown-up things.

"Let's play Popeye!" he cried, jumping up and down. "Let's play Teeny Mutant Stinky Turtles!" (He never gets that right.) "Let's go outside! Let's play on the swings!"

"Whew, hold it, Jamie," I said. "You're wearing me out, and I'm still sitting down. How about inviting a friend over?"

"I have a friend," said Jamie. "His name is Boris and he lives under the stairs. Want to meet him?"

"I meant a real friend."

"Boris is real!"

"Okay, a friend you can see, not an invisible one."

"We-ell . . ."

"Dawn is baby-sitting for the Perkins girls. Do you want to invite Myriah over? And maybe Gabbie?"

"Okay," replied Jamie, "but not Laura. She's another baby."

Laura did come over, though. That was because Dawn came over, so of course she brought all the girls with her. The Perkins family had moved into Kristy's old house, across the street from me. There are three Perkins girls. Myriah is five and a half, Gabbie is two and a half, and Laura is the baby. Jamie has become good friends with Myriah and Gabbie, and I can see why. They're lots of fun. They love to sing and dance and put on shows. And Myriah takes all kinds of lessons and classes — tap dancing, acting, singing. She and Gabbie know the words to lots of long songs. When Laura is older, she'll probably join her sisters in their acts. Right now she just watches them, cooing and smiling. (Sometimes I look at Lucy and Laura, who are practically the same age, and wonder if they'll grow up together and become best friends, like Mary Anne and Kristy did.)

When the Newtons' doorbell rang, Jamie

greeted our visitors with his call of, "Hi-hi! Hi-hi!"

"Hi-hi!" replied Dawn, Myriah, and Gabbie obediently.

"Hi-hi," I said to Dawn, and giggled.

We were about to take the five children into the Newtons' backyard when the phone rang. I dashed for it. "Hello, Newtons' residence," I said.

"Hi, Claud, it's me."

"Hi, Stace! What's going on?"

"The weather's so beautiful that even Charlotte wants to be out in it."

"No kidding." Stacey was baby-sitting at another house in the neighborhood, for eight-year-old Charlotte Johanssen. Charlotte is a wonderful kid — we all love her. She's quiet and sensitive (a little like Mary Anne), and extremely bright. She's already skipped a grade in school. Charlotte's main interests are reading and studying. (She has friends, though. Her very best friend is Becca Ramsey, Jessi's younger sister.) Anyway, Charlotte's request to play outside was a little unusual. "Come on over here," I said. "Dawn just came by with Myriah and Gabbie and Laura. Maybe Charlotte would like to play with the kids."

"Okay. Thanks. We'll walk Carrot over." Carrot is the Johanssens' schnauzer. He's getting a little fat. I mean, for a schnauzer.

No sooner had I hung up the phone than it rang again. "Sheesh," I mumbled. I picked up the receiver. "Hello, Newtons' residence."

"Hi, Claud."

"Mary Anne?"

"Yeah. I'm at the Hobarts'. I'm sitting for Mathew and Johnny."

The Hobarts have four boys. And they live in Mary Anne's old house! Mary Anne was watching the two younger Hobarts. (Mathew is six and Johnny is four. The oldest Hobart, Ben, is Mallory's very first boyfriend.) "So what are you doing?" Mary Anne asked.

"Dawn's here with the Perkins girls, and Stacey's on her way over with Charlotte. And Carrot."

"Oh. Darn. Johnny wanted Jamie to come over here."

"Why don't you bring the boys *here*? We'll have a play group."

"Awesome! We'll be right over."

Before I knew it, the Newtons' backyard was crawling with kids. (And one dog.) Jamie, Lucy, Myriah, Gabbie, Laura, Charlotte, Mathew, and Johnny. (And Carrot.)

My friends and I watched them for a few moments.

"Hey, you know what?" I cried suddenly. "You know what we have here?"

"A zoo?" suggested Stacey.

"No, a band. Or the beginnings of one. Lucy and Laura are too little, of course, and I don't know if Charlotte would want to be part of something like that, but here are five other kids."

"Yeah!" said Dawn. "Well, let's see what they think. Hey, you guys!" she called to the children swarming over Jamie's swingset.

"What?" Jamie called back.

"Come here!"

"Me?"

"All of you. We have an idea."

When the kids had gathered around us, my friends looked expectantly at me. "Um." I cleared my throat. "Would you guys like to be in a band?"

"Whose band?" asked Myriah.

"Yours. I mean, ours. We'll start our own band."

"What's a band?" Gabbie wanted to know.

Hmm. Good question. "Well, it's a group of people playing songs together on musical instruments," I replied.

"Are you going to teach us to play the instruments?" asked Jamie.

"Some of you," answered Stacey. "Some of you already play instruments."

"I play the violin," spoke up Mathew, proudly.

"I play the guitar," added Charlotte, sounding shy.

"You do? I didn't know that," said Stacey.

"I just started taking lessons. I was going to wait until I got good before I told anybody about it."

"You mean you'd want to be in the band?" said Mary Anne incredulously.

"I think so." Char's voice was a whisper, but she was smiling.

"Maybe the band should have some singers," suggested Myriah. "Gabbie and I are very good singers."

"I want to play the drums," said Johnny Hobart, "only I don't have any. We rented a violin for Mathew, but I don't have drums."

"Then we'll make some," said Mary Anne. "It's easy."

The kids were becoming excited.

"What could I play?" asked Jamie.

"We'll need more instruments," said Charlotte.

"How about some other band members?" I asked.

"Becca!" exclaimed Charlotte. "If I'm in the band, she's in the band."

"Maybe the Pike kids," suggested Stacey.

"Cool. We'll invite them over."

"Right now?" asked Mary Anne.

"Why not?"

Twenty minutes later the yard was even more jam-packed. The twelve of us had been joined by Jessi with Becca, and Mal with Nicky, Margo, and Claire, the three youngest Pikes. Nicky is eight, Margo is seven, and Claire is five.

I explained the band to its four newest members, and now all I could hear were cries of, "I want to play the tambourine!" "I want to play a harmonica!" "I want to make lots of noise!" (That was Nicky.) "Does anyone have a tuba?" (That was Claire, who has never played the tuba. "You don't even know what a tuba *looks* like," Margo said witheringly to her sister.)

Mary Anne, our dutiful club secretary, found a pencil and a memo pad in the Newtons' kitchen. She brought them into the backyard and began making notes: who wanted to sing, who wanted to play instruments, who *needed* instruments, and so forth.

"Someone should call Kristy and tell her what's going on," said Dawn.

"We should call the Rodowskys, too. After all, they gave me the idea for the band," I pointed out.

"We should probably call a lot of other kids," added Stacey. "We don't want to leave anyone out."

Mary Anne flipped to another page on the

memo pad and carefully wrote: KIDS TO CALL. We listed Kristy's younger brothers and sister, the Barretts, the Arnold twins, Jenny Prezzioso, Nina Marshall, and the Braddocks.

"Anyone else?" I asked during a lull in the activity.

"Maybe the Papadakis kids," said Dawn.

"How about the Lowells?" added Mary Anne. "Since they're new clients of the BSC, it might be nice to ask them to join. Anyway, I like the kids. For one thing, they're obedient. They'll be able to follow directions."

I grinned. "Good idea. I'm sitting at the Lowells' tomorrow, so I'll ask them then."

Mary Anne scribbled furiously on her pad.

CHAPTER 5

Mrs. Lowell had asked me to arrive at three-thirty the next afternoon. I didn't want to be late for my new job, so I raced directly to the Lowells' as soon as school let out. I didn't bother to go home first. As a result I was standing on the Lowells' front doorstep at exactly 3:19. Good, I thought. It can't hurt to show up early for new clients.

I pressed the doorbell and heard chimes ring in the house. When the door opened, I put on a bright smile. "Hi!" I said.

The woman standing in the entryway did not smile. And she hesitated before saying, "Hello. I'm Mrs. Lowell. Claudia?"

I nearly replied, "Yes, ma'am." Mrs. Lowell made me feel . . . formal. But my mouth had gone dry, so I just nodded.

Mrs. Lowell nodded back. "Well, come on inside." She walked away, leaving me to open the screen door and let myself inside. I followed her into the kitchen, trying to think of something to say.

The best I could come up with was, "Mary Anne really liked Caitlin and Mackie and Celeste. Um, are they here?"

"Caitlin and Mackie aren't home from school yet. Celeste is napping," was the reply. Mrs. Lowell looked everywhere but at me.

Suddenly I knew what was wrong. I'd eaten a bag of cashews on the way to the Lowells' house. I bet bits of nuts were stuck between my teeth. And Mrs. Lowell was so embarrassed for me she didn't know what to say. But I ran my tongue over my teeth and felt nothing. Hmm. Maybe my mascara had smeared. Or my hair was parted strangely. Or I had arrived *too* early after all.

"Claudia? Are you paying attention to me?" snapped Mrs. Lowell.

"Yes, ma'am." (Actually, I wasn't.)

"Our next-door neighbor is Mr. Selznick," she went on. "He's usually home during the day. You can call him in an emergency."

"Does he work at home?" I asked. (Maybe he was an artist.)

"What does it matter?"

I know I blushed then. I just know it. My face grew hot. It must have turned the color of a fire engine.

I shrugged and looked down. As I did, I caught sight of my black leggings and high-topped sneakers, my fringed blue-jean vest and beaded Indian belt, my six silver rings and . . .

Uh-oh. That was it. Mrs. Lowell didn't approve of my outfit. She thought it was too wild. It wasn't appropriate for her kids. That must be it. Mary Anne had written about the Lowell kids' clothes in the club notebook, how neatly and properly they were dressed, especially Caitlin and Mackie in their school uniforms. Of course, Mary Anne would have been neatly and properly dressed, too. She always is, thanks to her father. No wonder Mrs. Lowell didn't like me. And no wonder she had liked Mary Anne.

As Mrs. Lowell was finishing up her list of instructions, the front door burst open and then a girl and boy rushed into the kitchen.

"Hi, Mom!" cried the girl.

"Hi, Mommy!" cried the boy.

Mrs. Lowell's face softened into a warm smile. "Hi, kids. How was school? Come have a snack."

"But, Mom, who's *that*?" The girl was pointing at me.

"Caitlin, Mackie, this is your baby-sitter, Claudia Kishi," said Mrs. Lowell. She paused, then added, "Please be nice to her."

I forced a smile. "Hi, Caitlin. Hi, Mackie," I said.

Mackie said nothing, but Caitlin covered her mouth and giggled. I hoped that was a good sign.

"Well," said Mrs. Lowell presently, "I suppose I should go now." But she didn't. She couldn't seem to leave the room.

"Don't worry about Celeste," I said. "I mean, if you're afraid she'll be scared when she wakes up and finds a sitter here."

"No, it isn't that," said Mrs. Lowell vaguely.

So what *was* it?

I didn't find out. Mrs. Lowell finally managed to leave. Whew. Oh, well. I would only have to face her for a few more minutes at the end of the afternoon. In between I would have fun with the obedient, curious, and well-behaved children Mary Anne had liked so much.

Wrong.

The afternoon started off badly.

Caitlin and Mackie ate four Oreos each and reached for more. "Wait!" I cried. "That's enough!"

"We're hungry," said Caitlin, and grabbed a handful of cookies before I could put the package away.

She and her brother ate greedily, then

jumped up and ran out of the kitchen, leaving a crumb-covered table behind. I began to clean the kitchen while they shrieked through the house.

"Quiet!" I hissed.

They shrieked around until I could hear someone crying.

"Who's hurt?" I called.

"Nobody!" Mackie replied. "Celeste's awake!"

Well, no wonder. I dashed upstairs. "Caitlin, Mackie," I said, "please wipe the kitchen table while I get Celeste up."

The kids disappeared downstairs, then returned quickly.

"We have to talk to Celeste," Caitlin announced. "We have to tell her about her new baby-sitter."

Maybe that was a good idea. Celeste was still crying. She was probably confused. Her sister and brother would be able to calm her down. I stepped into the hallway, leaving the three kids in Celeste's room. Several minutes passed and the sound of crying faded away. I could hear only the low murmur of voices.

"Everything all right in there?" I called.

"Yup!" replied someone, probably Caitlin.

"Okay, then I'm coming in." When I returned to Celeste's room, she gazed at me from where she was sitting on her bed sandwiched between her brother and sister. And she didn't stop staring until Mackie nudged her in her side.

"Celeste, do you want a snack?" I asked.

She nodded. And Mackie cried, "Me, too!"

"You just had one," I reminded him.

"Well, I want another."

"So do I," added Caitlin.

"No way."

"I'll tell Mom you were a mean sitter," said Caitlin, eyes narrowed.

I stood before the Lowell children, trying to decide how to handle the situation. I remembered the time Stacey had tried something she called "reverse psychology" on the two bratty Delaney kids who used to live across the street from Kristy's new house. How had that worked? Had she told them to do the opposite of what she really wanted them to do? That sounded right.

"Okay," I said, "I guess you guys didn't have enough to eat before. You better try to finish off that package of cookies."

"The whole package?!" exclaimed Caitlin.

"Really? You mean it?" cried Mackie.

Uh-oh. Now what? This wasn't how Stacey's reverse psychology was supposed to work. I could picture what would happen that afternoon. The kids would gorge themselves with Oreos and be sick to their stomachs by the time their mother came home. That would be great, just great.

"Um," I began.

Ring, ring.

"Telephone! I'll get it!" shrieked Caitlin. She dashed out of Celeste's room. Several moments later I heard her call, "Claudia! For you!"

Caitlin handed me the extension in the hallway. It's probably Mrs. Lowell, I thought miserably. She's phoning to check up on me.

But the caller was Mary Anne.

"I'm at the Hobarts'," she said. "A whole bunch of us are here. We're planning the band. Do the Lowells want to join?"

"Oh, my gosh! I forgot to ask them. I think we'll just walk on over there so the kids can see what's going on. We need to get out of the house. We'll be there in a few minutes."

The Lowells forgot about the cookies when I told them we were going to take a walk and meet some new kids, and that they would get to see Mary Anne again. Soon we were milling around the Hobarts' backyard along with Myriah and Gabbie, who had run over from next door; Jamie Newton; Mallory with Nicky, Margo, and Claire; Kristy with David Michael, Karen, and Andrew; Stacey with Charlotte; Dawn with the Rodowsky boys; and Mary Anne with Jenny Prezzioso. A few other neighborhood kids had arrived, too.

The yard was full of noise and fun.

"I brought my kazoo," announced Jackie.

"I found a pair of tom-toms in our basement," said Haley Braddock. "Matt can play those because he can feel the beat." (Haley's brother Matt is profoundly deaf.)

Celeste spotted Mary Anne, ran to her, and clung to her hands (what was wrong with *me*?), but Mackie and Caitlin joyfully joined the other kids in planning the band and deciding what songs to learn. They had so much fun that when it was time to leave I hated to call them away. And believe me, they did not want to be called away.

"I don't *want* to leave!" cried Mackie.

"Maybe," said Caitlin, eyeing me, "Claudia will let us eat Oreos when we get home. We never got to eat our extras."

"No Oreos," I said. "It's too close to dinner now."

"But we're hungry!" said Mackie.

"Good, then you'll have plenty of room for your supper."

I walked the Lowell kids home (after I pried Celeste away from Mary Anne), and they whined and complained the entire way.

"You *prom*ised us Oreos," said Caitlin.

"I promised you Oreos when it was four o'clock. Now it's too late."

"Hmphh."

Back at the Lowells' house, I settled the kids into a game of Memory. They kept slipping out of the family room, though. One at a time. Soon I discovered what they were doing. Sneaking grapes.

"I said no snacking!" I cried.

"No, you didn't!" replied Mackie. "You said no Oreos."

I sighed.

I prayed for Mrs. Lowell's safe and quick return.

I couldn't get out of there fast enough.

CHAPTER 6

"Junk food, anyone?" I asked. I pulled a sack of Payday bars from the depths of one of my bureau drawers.

"Got any chips or Fritos?" asked Stacey.

"Or wheat germ biscuits?" asked Dawn.

"Oh, yeah. Right. Wheat germ biscuits. I have them hidden here under the bed along with my endless supply of tofu." (Dawn laughed.) "Will you settle for unsalted stone-ground wheat crackers?" I asked.

Dawn raised her eyebrows. "Sure!" she exclaimed.

"Me, too!" added Stacey. Then she frowned. "Oh, you're kidding. I get it. Silly me. For a moment, I thought — "

"No, I really do have them," I interrupted her. "I bought them just for you guys." I found the box of crackers on the floor under a pile of clean laundry. "Here we go," I said. "I aim to please."

It was 5:25 and another meeting of the BSC was about to begin. We were sitting comfortably in our usual places. Kristy was ensconced in the director's chair; Mary Anne and Stacey and I were lined up on my bed; Dawn was seated backward at the desk chair, her arms dangling over the top rung; and Jessi and Mal were curled up on the floor.

"Okay, please come to order," said Kristy when the food had been handed around and we were munching away.

We settled down. And right away the phone rang.

"I got it!" said Mal. "Hello, Baby-sitters Club. Mallory Pike speaking. . . . Hi, Mrs. Lowell. . . . Kristy? Okay, just a sec." Mallory put her hand over the receiver and said, "Kristy, Mrs. Lowell wants to talk to you."

"Okay," Kristy answered, frowning. She reached for the phone.

Requesting a particular sitter is not club policy.

"Maybe she isn't calling about a job," whispered Jessi.

"That must be it," I agreed.

But Kristy's end of the conversation certainly sounded work-related. "Two hours?" she said. Then she went on, "But — Well, okay. I mean, that isn't . . . um, did something happen? Why don't you want . . ."

I looked at Kristy. Her eyes were downcast. She seemed to be studying her sneakers. So I looked at the rest of my friends. They were exchanging puzzled glances.

Finally Kristy said, "I'll call you right back, okay?"

"What was that all about?" I asked as soon as she'd hung up.

"I'll explain in a few minutes," Kristy replied. "Who's free on Wednesday afternoon, Mary Anne?"

"This Wednesday? Let me see. . . . Just Jessi."

"Want to sit for the Lowells, Jessi?" asked Kristy.

"Sure. Why not?"

Kristy called Mrs. Lowell back, then faced the rest of us BSC members, looking serious. "I have to tell you this," she said, "and I might as well tell you straight out. When Mrs. Lowell called, she said she needed a sitter, but she asked for someone besides Claudia."

I gasped. "What?" I whispered.

Kristy shook her head. "I don't understand it, but that's what she said. Did anything happen when you were there, Claud? If it did, you should have told me about it."

"There's nothing to tell. It wasn't my best sitting job ever, but nothing horrible happened. Nobody got hurt, nothing was broken."

"Is one of the Lowells a walking disaster like Jackie Rodowsky?" asked Jessi. She looked worried. I knew she was beginning to wonder about the job she'd just accepted.

"No! Not at all. Think of the horrible things that have happened when we've sat for Jackie. Broken vases, grape juice on the carpet, skinned knees, banged heads. The Lowells were angels compared to Jackie." I felt numb. And I was angry that I had to defend myself when nothing had happened.

"The Lowells *are* sort of angelic, aren't they?" said Mary Anne.

I paused. "Actually, I didn't have quite the experience with them that you did," I said after a moment.

"Wait. I'm confused, Claudia," said Kristy. "Were the Lowells okay or not? What did go on when you sat for them?"

"Well, nothing. But something." Kristy looked very frustrated, so I rushed on. "Okay. The kids and I didn't really get along. Remember the Delaneys? Well, Caitlin and Mackie reminded me of Amanda and Max Delaney."

"You know, they *do* sort of look like them," spoke up Mary Anne.

"I mean they acted like them. They wouldn't

obey me. They tried to get away with things. They snuck food before dinner. When I set limits, they said they were going to tell on me, tell their mom I was mean to them or something."

"You should have let me know," Kristy said again.

"Well, I wrote about it in the notebook," I pointed out. "And anyway, like I said, none of the things that happened seemed that bad. No broken lamps, no grape juice stains, not even a skinned knee."

Now Mary Anne was frowning. "The kids were perfect when I sat for them. They did everything I suggested. And when Mrs. Lowell came home she kept smiling and telling me what a wonderful job I'd done and commenting on how happy the kids looked."

"What did I do wrong? Maybe the kids *really* spoiled their appetites when they snuck that food."

"What did they eat?" asked Stacey.

"Some grapes."

"That's *it*? Some grapes? You mean a couple of bunches?"

"No. Just a few grapes each. I checked the fruit bowl."

"That wouldn't spoil their appetites," said Dawn. "I thought you meant they raided the cookie jar."

"Nope. But maybe they have small stomachs. Or maybe the problem is something totally different. Maybe the kids told their mother they didn't have fun at the Hobarts'."

"Oh, they had a great time," said Mary Anne. "I was watching them."

"Then maybe Mrs. Lowell didn't like my taking them somewhere else to play. But she didn't say not to leave the yard."

"And the Hobarts are so close by," added Jessi.

"Maybe she doesn't like the Hobarts?" I wondered.

"I don't think the Lowell kids had ever *met* the Hobarts before," said Mallory. "I don't think they knew any of the kids there."

"I know! Mrs. Lowell didn't like my outfit!" I exclaimed. "I forgot about that. I'm positive she was looking at it and she thought it was too wild, especially considering what Caitlin and Mackie and Celeste were wearing."

"But why didn't she just say so?" asked Dawn.

I shrugged. So did Kristy.

"Well, I *did* get there a little early," I said after a moment.

"That's no reason to ask you not to sit again," Kristy pointed out.

Mr. Ohdner phoned then, needing a sitter. And then several more clients called. Our meeting became very busy. We couldn't talk about the Lowells again until nearly six o'clock.

"I hope," I said, "that you all noticed no one else asked me not to sit for them. Did you notice that?"

Kristy smiled. "I'm sorry if I sounded like I was accusing you before, but Mrs. Lowell was so clear about not wanting you to sit. The only logical explanation was that something had happened. Maybe I should phone Mrs. Lowell and talk to her tonight. I feel funny about that, though. And anyway, she does want to keep using the BSC," said Kristy.

"Maybe I'll find out something when I sit," said Jessi.

"Dress nicely," I advised her. "And keep the kids at home."

"Okay," agreed Jessi solemnly. Then she grinned. "I'll keep them out of the grapes, too."

CHAPTER 7

Wednesday

I don't really see the point in writing up my "job" at the Lowells' yesterday, since there was no job after all. But a rule is a rule, so I'll write it up anyway. Here is what happened: nothing. I didn't get past the front door. Okay. Is everybody satisfied with my entry?

Later:

Sorry, you guys. I didn't mean to sound angry at you. Because I'm not. I'm angry at Mrs. Lowell, I guess, but I don't even know why.

After that weird club meeting, the one during which Mrs. Lowell phoned and requested any baby-sitter *except* me, Jessi decided she ought to be better prepared than usual when she met her new sitting charges. She wanted the afternoon to go perfectly so that Mrs. Lowell wouldn't be able to find a single fault with Jessi's work.

Jessi planned carefully. When the meeting was over she ran home, and after dinner she opened her Kid-Kit and examined the contents.

"Hmm. Low on crayons," she murmured. "And not enough books for little kids. I better find some that Celeste will like." Jessi removed a couple of items from the kit (to make room for more books), and wandered into her family's rec room. From a shelf, she pulled *Blueberries For Sal*, *The Snowy Day*, *A Chair For My Mother*, and *Good Dog, Carl*. She placed them by the kit.

Now, she thought, do I have enough toys for six-year-old boys? The kit was stocked with plenty of art materials (good for boys and girls of all ages), some easy jigsaw puzzles, and a bunch of Matchbox cars and trucks.

"Now for eight-year-old girls," muttered Jessi, and she marched upstairs to her sister's room.

58

"Becca?"

"Yeah?" Jessi's sister was sitting at her desk, writing something on a sheet of paper with wide lines on it.

"What are you doing?" asked Jessi.

"My homework. We're supposed to write a story called 'The Ghost in My Room.' It has to be two pages long." Becca looked pained.

"That sounds like fun!" exclaimed Jessi. "Listen, Becca, I have to put some stuff in my Kid-Kit that eight-year-old girls will especially like. Do you have any ideas?"

"Barbies," said Becca, without looking up from her paper. "And stickers. Oh, and Charlotte and I like to play office."

"Great, Becca. Thanks," said Jessi.

What a terrific idea! Jessi decided to put together an office package for Caitlin. Before she did that, though, she phoned Mary Anne. "I'm getting ready for my job at the Lowells'," she told her. "I want to make sure I have special stuff in my Kid-Kit for each of the children. And guess what Becca suggested. She said Caitlin might like to play office. What do you think?"

"I think that sounds great. I mean, we didn't play office when I baby-sat, but I'm sure Caitlin would like that game."

"Okay. I'm going to make up an office set for her."

It took Jessi half an hour (when she should have been working on an assignment for her French class), but finally she had filled a plastic box with colored pencils, Magic Markers, pens, erasers, paper clips (red, white, and blue), blunt scissors, tape, memo pads, rubber bands, stickers, animal stamps, writing paper, and envelopes.

"There," she said. "Boy. I should win the Best Baby-sitter Award.

On the day of her job at the Lowells', Jessi made sure to arrive exactly five minutes early — early enough to make a good impression, but not so early as to annoy Mrs. Lowell (in case that's what I had done). Jessi was determined to please her new clients.

Jessi paused on the Lowells' front stoop, clutching her Kid-Kit. She pictured the office set tucked inside. She was pretty sure Caitlin would like it. Jessi had shown it to Becca the night before, and Becca not only had fallen in love with it, but had begged her sister to put together one just for her — which Jessi had done.

Jessi drew in a breath and pressed the bell.

A few moments later the door swung open.

Jessi smiled at the woman standing before her. "Hi," she said. "I'm Jessi Ramsey. I'm the baby-sitter."

Mrs. Lowell looked shocked. When Jessi told us her story that afternoon, that was the only word she used to describe the expression on Mrs. Lowell's face. "Shocked," Jessi repeated to us. "I don't know how else to put it."

Mrs. Lowell stared at Jessi for a full six seconds and, during that time, Jessi did just what I had done when Mrs. Lowell and I faced each other. She tried to figure out what could possibly be wrong with what Mrs. Lowell saw. Had she buttoned her shirt crookedly? Were her jeans unzipped? Wait! Maybe Mrs. Lowell expected girls to wear dresses. . . . No. Jessi knew that Caitlin and Celeste owned blue jeans. Nervously, Jessi glanced down at herself, then back at Mrs. Lowell.

"Did — did I come at the wrong time?" Jessi stammered, checking her watch.

"No, um . . . No." Mrs. Lowell took a step backward. "I don't need a sitter after all," she finally managed to say. "I forgot to tell you."

Mrs. Lowell closed the front door.

Jessi remained motionless on the stoop. She felt like crying, although she wasn't quite sure why. She hadn't been yelled at or scolded or injured. Yet she was hurt. And a familiar thought nagged at her but wouldn't make itself known.

Jessi turned around slowly and walked

down the Lowells' driveway. When she reached the sidewalk she turned around and looked at the house. She couldn't see anyone; not Mrs. Lowell, not the children. Just a curtain moving near a window by the front door.

The Wednesday afternoon meeting of the BSC wouldn't begin for almost two hours. Jessi, carrying the Kid-Kit, walked toward Mallory's house. For some reason she didn't feel like going home and telling anyone what had just happened at the Lowells'. Jessi scuffed down the street thinking of the office set she'd made for Caitlin, of the half hour she *should* have spent doing her homework.

By the time she reached the Pikes' house she was crying.

But by the time she and Mal arrived in BSC headquarters, she had stopped. She simply looked puzzled — as puzzled as I still felt.

"Maybe Mrs. Lowell expected someone older," suggested Jessi when the meeting was underway. "Maybe she thought I would be thirteen, like Mary Anne and Claudia."

"But why wouldn't she just have said so?" asked Kristy, who was scowling under her visor. Clearly, she thought Mrs. Lowell was Trouble. I could tell she was trying to figure out what to do about her. Clients must be handled delicately.

"I don't know. She looked embarrassed,"

replied Jessi. "Well, no, that's not true. Like I said, she mostly looked shocked. And you know what? She practically slammed the door in my face!"

I gave Jessi a sympathetic glance. Then, to make her feel better, I asked her to show us the office kit she had put together. We all exclaimed over it, and about half of us decided to put together kits of our own.

But we could not forget about Mrs. Lowell.

"Maybe she'll call during the meeting," said Kristy.

She didn't. Each time the phone rang we looked at it expectantly. Once Dawn even said, staring at the receiver, "I *will* you to be Mrs. Lowell." The caller was Mr. Hobart.

"I guess I could phone Mrs. Lowell," said Kristy uncertainly. "In fact, I probably ought to. As club president, it's my job to find out if we have a dissatisfied client."

"Hey!" exclaimed Jessi, brightening. "Wait a sec! We're making too much of this. Maybe Mrs. Lowell really *did* forget she didn't need a sitter. Her plans changed and she forgot to call us to cancel. So she was embarrassed."

"I don't know," I said, not wanting to deflate Jessi, but wanting to be honest with her. "That doesn't explain why she never wants *me* to sit for her kids again."

Jessi sagged. "True."

For several minutes the seven of us sat in silence. At last Mary Anne sighed, then said, "Well, I'm supposed to sit for the Lowells again next week. Should we wait and see how that goes?"

"Sure," Kristy answered. "Why not? I don't know what else to do."

The clock turned to six and Kristy adjourned the meeting. My friends wandered quietly out of my room, through the hall, down the stairs, out the front door.

At dinner, I tried to be cheerful.

CHAPTER 8

"You know what we need?" asked Jackie Rodowsky. "We need a name. That's what. And it should be, like, catchy."

Jackie was talking about the band. My friends and I had managed to get the kids together several times and, by now, everyone had chosen whether to be a singer or a player, the players had decided on instruments, and the instruments had been either found or made. The band was heavy on kazoos and percussion (a lot of the littler kids had insisted on playing drums, tambourines, sticks, and cymbals), but we also featured a couple of piano players, a flute player, a trumpet player, a violin player, and Charlotte, our guitar player. Myriah, Gabbie, Buddy Barrett, and Margo Pike were our singers.

At our first band practice, the kids had unanimously voted to learn the song "Tomorrow" from the musical *Annie*.

65

Now, sitting for the Rodowskys one Saturday, the boys were rehearsing — and Jackie had decided the band needed a name.

"You know you're right," I replied. "Any suggestions, Jackie?"

Jackie bit his lip and stared into space. He fiddled with his kazoo. "How about the Beatles?"

"I think that's been taken."

"The Little Beatles? The Baby Beatles?"

"Your name should say more about *you*."

"Jackie Rodowsky's All-Star Orchestra!"

"It isn't *your* band, Jackie," said Archie indignantly.

And Shea added, "*I* think the name should be funny."

"String Beans!" said Archie.

"Turtle Toes!" said Shea.

I giggled. "Come on, you guys."

The Rodowsky boys grew quiet, thinking. After a moment Jackie said seriously, "You know what? I think we should call ourselves All the Children, like short for All the Children of the World. Because we *are* all kids, and we're all different kinds of kids; different ages, different colors — "

"Yeah!" said Shea, catching on. "And our families come from all different countries. We're Polish," he said proudly.

"And I'm Japanese," I added. "And Hannie

and Linny Papadakis are Greek, and the Hobarts are Australian."

"Did you know," spoke up Archie, "that Jamie Newton's great-great-great-grandfather was an Indian? So Jamie is a real, true American, because the Indians lived in America before anyone else did. And they're called Native Americans now. My teacher said so."

"Well I like All the Children," I said. "It's a great name for the band."

"I like it, too," said Shea and Archie at the same time.

Jackie grinned, pleased with himself.

"Okay, are you guys ready to rehearse?" I asked. "I think we should have our own practice before we go to Jamie's for the big practice." Our band had been rehearsing at the Newtons' because Mr. and Mrs. Newton had been nice enough to say that not only could our two piano players use their electric keyboard, but that we could set it up on their back porch, since it was easier for the band to play outdoors.

"Claudia?" said Jackie. "When we go to Jamie's, can we tell the other kids the name for our band?"

"Of course," I answered. "Except I don't think we should *tell* the kids. I think they should vote on it. Just to be democratic. Now, are you guys ready to rehearse?"

"We better warm up, first," said Archie.

The boys ran into the living room where I could see a tambourine sitting on the piano. Shea slid onto the piano bench, Archie grabbed the tambourine, and Jackie held up his kazoo.

"Scales!" ordered Shea. He placed his thumb on middle C and accompanied himself while he sang, "Do re mi fa sol la ti do."

Jackie played along, humming off-key.

Archie beat the tambourine in time to the piano.

"Fantastic!" proclaimed Shea when they had finished. "Okay, everybody. Get ready for 'Tomorrow.' Claudia, you sing."

"Me? Sing the *song*?" I asked, my voice squeaking.

"Yeah. It helps me keep my place. Besides, we're used to hearing Myriah and Gabbie and everyone sing while we play."

"But I *can't* sing. I have an awful voice." (Actually, my voice isn't all that bad, but I hadn't memorized the words to the song.)

"Oh, anyone can sing," said Shea.

"Not me."

"I'll sing then," said Archie.

Shea looked suspiciously at his youngest brother. "Are you sure you know the words?" he asked.

"Sure I'm sure. Let's start."

"Ready, guys? I'll count you off," I said. "One, two, three, four."

Shea's fingers hit the keys, Jackie blew seriously into his kazoo, and Archie beat the tambourine and sang, "The sun'll come out tomorrow. Bet your bell bottoms tomorrow there'll be — "

Shea stopped playing. "Excuse me?"

"What?" said Archie.

Jackie cracked up. "You said 'Bet your bell bottoms'!"

"All right, we won't have a singer," said Shea, sighing dramatically.

"Then can I have a tambourine solo?" Archie wanted to know.

"NO!" cried Shea.

He was clearly frustrated, but the rehearsal had to stop for awhile anyway when Jackie dropped his kazoo into the piano.

"You know what?" I said when the kazoo had been recovered. "It's time to go to Jamie's. Jackie, Archie, remember your instruments. Shea, remember your music."

The Rodowsky boys and I set out for the walk to the Newtons'. We could hear our band long before we could see it. From several houses away drifted toots and beeps and jingles and crashes and plinks and shouts and laughs and giggles.

69

"Hello, everybody!" called Jackie as we stepped through the gate in the Newtons' fence. "We have great news!"

"What is it?" asked Kristy and, one by one, heads turned toward us.

Jackie stepped forward. "I thought of a name for our band," he said. "I think we should call ourselves All the Children, because we are sort of like all the children of the world."

For just a moment I thought some of the kids, especially the older ones, might give him a hard time. But they just began to smile. I glanced at Kristy and she was smiling, too. So were the other members of the BSC. I put my arm around Jackie.

"I guess that's settled," said Kristy. "Okay. Who are we missing today?" She gazed around the yard.

We ran our rehearsals loosely. Anyone who was free was expected to show up. Anyone who wasn't free was simply supposed to try to show up at the next rehearsal. That afternoon, the Lowell kids were missing. So were the Barretts, Linny Papadakis, and David Michael Thomas. Even so, we were left with a fairly impressive band and three of our four singers.

"Okay, kids," I said. "Places!"

In the scramble that followed, Claire Pike

fell and bumped her knees, Archie managed to sit on his tambourine (without breaking it), Hannie Papadakis lost her harmonica, and two kids announced that they had shown up for rehearsal without their drums. So Mal soothed her sister, Mary Anne helped Archie and Hannie, and Kristy said, "How could you come to a *band* rehearsal without your *in*struments?"

The kids shrugged.

"Kristy?" said Jamie. "Mommy put some empty coffee cans in the garage. We could use them for drums today."

So we did.

Then, "Places, everyone!" I called again.

I turned to Marilyn Arnold and Shea at the keyboard. "One, two — "

"Hey!" We were interrupted by Karen Brewer, Kristy's sister, who looked extremely excited. "You know what our band needs now?" she cried. "Since we have a name, we need to paint our name on one of our big drums. All the best bands do that. We would look so awesome. A huge round drum that said ALL THE CHILDREN."

"But we don't have a huge round drum," pointed out Myriah. "Our drums are oatmeal cartons and coffee cans."

"Oh, yeah." Karen looked disappointed.

"I suppose," I said, "that we could write ALL THE CHILDREN on the lids of the oatmeal cartons, but no one would see that."

"I have an idea," spoke up Mary Anne. "How about if we make a banner with our name? We could make a really long one."

"Out of felt," I added. "We could cut out the letters and glue them onto a piece of background material."

"Pink and white!" cried Karen.

"Those are *girl* colors," said Nicky Pike. "How about blue and white?"

"*Boy* colors!" countered Karen.

"You guys, we need to re*hearse*," Kristy broke in.

"And then, when we have our banner, we should give a show," said Jackie. "For our families and friends."

"We really need — " began Kristy.

"A musical program!" said Becca Ramsey.

"With *lots* of songs," added Charlotte Johanssen.

"We haven't even learned one song," muttered Kristy.

"We could play all the songs from *Annie*!" exclaimed Myriah.

"Yeah. We know the words," said Gabbie.

"There's 'Maybe' and 'The Hard-Knock Life' and 'You're Never Fully Dressed Without a Smile' and 'Little Girls,' " said Myriah.

"I am not going to play a song called 'Little Girls,' " said Nicky.

"How about playing 'Tomorrow'?" asked Kristy loudly. "Right now."

The kids stopped and stared at her.

"Oh, yeah. Our rehearsal," said Jackie.

"Shea? Marilyn?" I said. "One, two, three, four."

"The sun'll come out tomorrow!"

CHAPTER 9

Thursday

I baby-sat at the Lowells' house, and my afternoon there was interesting (to be polite). I mean, basically everything was fine. The kids were good. I didn't have any trouble with them, Claud. In fact, it was just a regular, normal old baby-sitting job. But the experience was sort of like a rotten Easter egg. It looks pretty on the outside, but you sure don't want to find out what's under the shell.

When I first read Kristy's notebook entry I got all huffy. Okay. So Mary Anne had had no trouble with the Lowell kids, and Kristy had had no trouble with them, but I could barely handle them. What did that say about me? That I was all washed up as a baby-sitter? That I was as *talentless* on the job as I was in school?

That's what I thought at first. Then I calmed down and read on.

Kristy was not even supposed to baby-sit for the Lowells'. Mary Anne was scheduled for the Thursday afternoon job. But Kristy's curiosity about Mrs. Lowell finally got the better of her. She decided she *had* to know why Mrs. Lowell was so short with me, and why she turned Jessi away. So she asked Mary Anne if she'd mind giving up her job. She even offered Mary Anne the money she would earn.

"Oh, you don't have to do that, Kristy," said Mary Anne. "Go ahead and see if Mrs. Lowell minds if you and I switch. I want to know what's going on, too. Anyway, maybe I'll get another job for Thursday. We've been so busy lately."

So Kristy phoned Mrs. Lowell. "Hello," she said. "This is Kristy Thomas. I'm the president of the Baby-sitters Club. We've talked on the phone before. Um, Mrs. Lowell, Mary Anne won't be able to baby-sit for you on Thursday. Something came up." (This was not, technically, a lie. Something *had* come up. Kristy wanted to meet Mrs. Lowell, that was what.) "But if it's all right with you, I can take her place. I'm thirteen, like Mary Anne, and I'm a very responsible sitter. Everyone says so."

"We-ell," said Mrs. Lowell, "all right. I'll be in a bind if I don't have a sitter on Thursday, so I guess it will be okay."

A brief silence followed, and Kristy sensed that Mrs. Lowell wanted to say something more. When she didn't, Kristy said, "So . . . good-bye, Mrs. Lowell. See you on Thursday."

"Good-bye."

Ding-dong.

Thursday had arrived and Kristy was at the Lowells' front door. Her heart pounded as she waited for Mrs. Lowell to open it.

Kristy wasn't taking any chances. Like Jessi, she arrived *exactly* five minutes early; no more, no less. And she was wearing a skirt. For Kristy, this was a supreme sacrifice. Ordinarily, she wears dresses or skirts only for special occasions, or if her mother makes her. But to go to the Lowells', Kristy put on a Mary Anne type of outfit — skirt, blouse, knee socks, loafers, even a ribbon in her hair.

Sure enough, when Mrs. Lowell answered the door, she did just what she'd done to Mary Anne and Jessi and me. She eyed Kristy — just for a moment. Then she smiled and invited her inside.

Kristy got the nice treatment, the Mary Anne treatment. This was good because after Mrs. Lowell had shown Kristy the emergency numbers and given her special instructions, Kristy felt comfortable enough to say, "Mrs. Lowell, since you're a new client of the Babysitters Club, may I ask you a very important question? About the quality of our service?"

"Certainly." Mrs. Lowell smiled.

"Are you satisfied with us so far? Are we doing a good job?"

"Oh, I'm quite pleased."

"Pleased with Mary Anne Spier?"

"Definitely."

"Pleased with Claudia Kishi?"

"She did a perfectly adequate job."

"But you don't want her to sit for you again?"

Mrs. Lowell's voice came out in a croak: "It's just that the children simply adore Mary Anne."

"And Jessi — "

"Mackie!" Mrs. Lowell called suddenly. "Caitlin! Is that you?"

"Yup, it's me. Hi, Mommy!"

"Hi, Mom!" added Caitlin.

The kids ran into the kitchen and Mrs. Lowell focused her attention on them. Kristy didn't have another chance to ask her about Jessi. But that didn't stop her from asking the kids questions.

Later, when Celeste had awakened from her nap, and she and Caitlin and Mackie were eating a snack with their new baby-sitter, Kristy said, "Do you guys like being in the band?"

"Yup," said Caitlin and Mackie.

"I like playing my sticks," added Celeste. "I am good at that."

"Did you know the band has a name now?" asked Kristy.

"It does?" replied Mackie. "What?"

"All the Children."

Caitlin nodded. "Very nice."

"I wish you guys could come more often," said Kristy. (The Lowell kids missed more rehearsals than they attended.)

"Mommy says she wants to see what we do there," Caitlin informed Kristy. "She hasn't met the kids yet."

"What do you mean?"

"You know. She likes to know who we're playing with."

"Oh." Kristy nodded. That made sense. Her mom and Watson liked to get to know the friends of her younger brothers and sisters.

"You're a nice baby-sitter," Mackie said a moment later.

"Thanks," replied Kristy. "I'm glad your mom calls our club. What do you think of your other sitters?"

"Mary Anne is fun!" said Caitlin. "She played games with us."

"I bet you liked Claudia, too. She's the one who helped you join the band. Remember? She took you to the Hobarts'."

"Oh, yeah," said Caitlin, and giggled. "She's the funny-looking one."

(Well, thanks a lot.)

For a moment, Kristy was confused. If I do say so myself, I am one of the more sophisticated kids at SMS. Everyone agrees. And one boy at school, Pete Black, has even said I'm awesome-looking. They say that about Stacey, too. It's pretty much accepted that both of us are way cool.

Which was why Kristy paused at the "funny-looking" comment. Then she thought about my clothes — and remembered why she herself was wearing a skirt that afternoon. That must be what Caitlin meant. My clothes and jewelry were too wild for the Lowells' taste.

"You know something weird?" Kristy went on. "Your mom hired another baby-sitter that

I don't think you guys even saw."

"Did she come really, really late at night?" Mackie wondered.

"Nope. She came in the afternoon."

"What does she look like?" asked Caitlin. "Maybe we did see her."

"Well, she's a dancer. She wears her hair pulled back. Her legs are really long. Um, she's African-American — "

Caitlin and Mackie were both drinking juice at that moment, and they nearly choked. "Well," said Caitlin scornfully, coughing, "I guess Mommy didn't like her." At least, that's what Kristy thought she said. But Caitlin was coughing so hard she might have said, "I guess that's why Mommy didn't like her."

Kristy couldn't stop thinking about the Lowells. She thought about them while her brother Charlie drove her home late that afternoon. And she thought about them during dinner.

"Kristy?" said her mother as they were clearing the table. "Are you all right? You're awfully quiet."

"Quiet for Kristy, or quiet for a normal person?" asked Sam.

Mrs. Brewer gave her son a Look.

Kristy barely heard him. "Mom, can we talk? Tonight?"

"Of course, honey. Girl talk?"

"No. Just serious talk. Can Nannie and Watson talk with us?"

"Whoa!" exclaimed Sam, and he whistled softly. "This must be *major*. What did you *do*?"

"Nothing."

"I'll find Nannie and Watson," said Kristy's mother.

"Are you flunking something?" asked Sam.

"Let's go in the living room, honey."

"Did you break something?" persisted Sam. "Steal something? Tell a lie?"

Kristy followed her mother into the living room. When Watson and her grandmother had joined them, she said, "What I'm going to say sounds awful, and I don't have any proof, but I *have* to talk to an adult. It's about the Lowells."

"Go ahead," said Mrs. Brewer.

"I think they're, um, racists."

"That's a pretty strong word," said Watson.

Kristy nodded. "I know. But Mrs. Lowell wouldn't let Jessi in their house, and the kids call Claudia 'the funny-looking one'. At first I thought they meant her clothes, but I have this horrible feeling they meant her — her face. Her eyes. They mean she's Asian." Kristy explained about our jobs with the Lowells.

When she finished speaking, she saw her mother and stepfather and grandmother looking worriedly at one another. Finally Nannie sighed and said, "With each generation I think it's going to be over. But it isn't even getting better. Maybe I'm just an old fool."

"The Lowells are the foolish ones, Nannie," said Kristy.

"Those poor children," murmured Mrs. Brewer. "They aren't even given the chance to make up their minds for themselves."

Watson nodded. "The sins of the fathers, et cetera."

"You know what?" said Kristy, her lower lip trembling. "I was hoping I was wrong. I was hoping you guys would tell me I was imagining things. Or being too dramatic or something."

"Oh, honey," said Mrs. Brewer. "I'd like to do that. Parents want to protect their children from everything that's bad. But they can't."

Kristy rested her head on her mother's shoulder. "Maybe I am wrong, though."

CHAPTER 10

"I guess," began Kristy, "that you guys are wondering what's going on."

I nodded.

"Yes," replied Jessi and Mal and Dawn.

"We need to talk about Mrs. Lowell," said Kristy.

I felt as if a block of ice had been dropped in my stomach. Something was very wrong. Kristy had been quiet at school that day, even during lunch. Now she was sitting in my director's chair, conducting a club meeting, but she'd forgotten to put on her presidential visor. And instead of sticking her pencil over her ear, she was toying nervously with it in her lap, twisting it in and out of her fingers.

Mrs. Lowell. Kristy had taken Mary Anne's sitting job at the Lowells' the day before. What had happened. What had Mrs. Lowell said? I was convinced I was in trouble.

Kristy bit her lip.

"What is it, Kristy?" asked Stacey. "What's wrong?"

Kristy looked so uncomfortable that I decided to save her from further torture. "I guess it's my fault. I blew my job at the Lowells and they've decided not to use the club anymore, right?" I said. "It's okay, Kristy. Just come out and say it."

Kristy couldn't look up. "That isn't exactly what's going on. But I guess I am trying to spare your feelings, Claud. Look, you guys. I think I made a horrible discovery. I talked about it with Mom and Watson and Nannie last night, and they think I might be right. The worst thing is, if I *am* right, we can't *do* anything."

"Kristy, please just tell me what — " Dawn began.

"The Lowells are prejudiced," said Kristy in a rush. "Claud, they didn't like you because you're Japanese. Jessi, Mrs. Lowell wouldn't even let you in her house because you're African-American."

My mouth dropped open. "But I'm a good baby-sitter!" I protested. I could feel my hands trembling and my cheeks burning. "That's — that's not fair! It really isn't fair." I looked at Jessi who was sitting cross-legged on the floor with Mallory. She wasn't saying anything.

84

"Jessi, aren't you mad?" I demanded. "At least Mrs. Lowell let me in the house. She closed her door to you."

"It's happened before," said Jessi quietly.

"Well, not to me!" I cried. For some reason I felt ashamed and I had the uncomfortable feeling that Kristy, Mary Anne, Mallory, Stacey, and Dawn felt ashamed *for* Jessi and me. "So — so what does being Asian have to do with being a good sitter?" I sputtered.

"Nothing," replied Jessi. "Prejudice doesn't make sense."

"It isn't rational or logical," added Mary Anne.

I was growing angry. The ice in my stomach had turned into a flame and now it was rising up, filling me, surrounding me. The problem was that I didn't know who to be angry at, since Mrs. Lowell wasn't in the room. Finally I got angry at my friends. "Will you guys at least *look* at me?" I shouted. "I am not dirt, you know. Nothing is *wrong* with me."

"Mrs. Lowell thinks we'll contaminate her children — and her house," said Jessi bitterly.

"Yeah, Mrs. *Low*ell thinks that," said Stacey pointedly.

"Sorry," I muttered.

"If it's any consolation," said Dawn, "I bet the Lowells don't like Jews or Indians or

Buddhists or Puerto Ricans or anyone who isn't white and just like their *perfect* family."

"Well, I'm not sure it's comforting to know I'm not the only one the Lowells hate — " I started to say.

"Claud, they don't hate you," spoke up Jessi. "They just don't understand you. That's the way my dad explained it to me once."

"What do they have to under*stand*?" I cried, still outraged. "I have two eyes, two ears, a nose, and a mouth, just like the Lowells. I live in a house like the Lowells' house. I have a family like the Lowells. My parents go to work and my sister and I go to school and when we get hungry we eat and when we get tired we sleep and we laugh and cry and fall in love. Just like the Lowells."

"Same here," said Jessi, "but my skin is black. And your eyes slant, Claud."

"So what?"

"That's why prejudice isn't rational."

"It must be hard to grow old," said Kristy.

I looked at her in confusion. "What?"

"Something Nannie said last night. She said she expected racism to decrease with each generation — or something like that — and that she's disappointed because things *aren't* getting better."

"Well, it does seem like things *used* to be worse," said Mallory hesitantly. "For hundreds of years African-Americans were kept as slaves. And during the Second World War the Nazis killed Jews and Catholics. But things are better now . . . aren't they?"

"Ever heard of the skinheads?" asked Stacey. "They beat up on people who are black or middle eastern or — or lots of things. And they live right here in the United States. Today. Same with the KKK."

"The what?" I frowned.

"The Ku Klux Klan," Jessi supplied. "They still exist. And not just in the south. In the north. In cities. In lots of places."

Mary Anne's eyes had filled with tears. "This is scary," she whispered. "I wonder if those skinheads could get *me* for anything. I think maybe some of my ancestors were Russian. I wonder if that's a problem."

"Ooh, now I understand what Nannie meant," said Mallory. "I guess as long as there's prejudice and misunderstanding, there's trouble. And innocent people worry and get hurt."

"Or killed," added Dawn.

Shame, anger, now fear. My feelings were jumbled up.

The phone rang then, and I jumped. I'd completely forgotten we were in a BSC meeting.

Jessi picked up the receiver. "Hello, Baby-sitters Club." She listened for a moment and her face became a mask. "Just a minute," she said coldly. "You can talk to Kristy." Jessi handed the phone across the room. "It's Mrs. Lowell," she said in a tone of voice I'd never heard her use. "I thought you might want to talk to her."

Kristy nodded. "Hello?" she said. And then, "I'll call you back."

"Why are you going to call her back?" I exploded as Kristy hung up the phone. "I was waiting for you to blow her off."

"So was *I*," replied Kristy, "but she took me by surprise. I couldn't think of what to say. Listen to this. Mrs. Lowell actually had the nerve just now to ask for the blonde-haired, blue-eyed baby-sitter she's heard about. Can you believe it? Who does she think we are? Who does she think I am? She knows *I'm* not blonde-haired and blue-eyed. Does she mean I'm not good enough to sit for her again?"

"See, Claudia?" spoke up Mary Anne. "I guess I wasn't such a hot baby-sitter after all. Mrs. Lowell isn't asking for me again either. Now you don't have to feel so bad."

Kristy was wearing a small smile. "You guys?" she said. "What are we going to do? When you think about it, this is sort of funny."

"Hysterical," I said.

Stacey, looking huffy, added, "I'm blonde-haired and blue-eyed and you wouldn't catch me dead sitting for the Lowells."

"Ditto," said Dawn.

By then, Kristy was grinning. "Perfect. Okay, watch this," she said. I couldn't help smiling a little myself. Kristy was up to something, and I knew it would be good.

Kristy phoned Mrs. Lowell back. "I'm sorry," she told her. "We're all out of blonde-haired, blue-eyed baby-sitters. And everyone else is busy. Oh, except for one of our associate members. His name is Logan." Kristy paused, apparently because she'd been cut off by Mrs. Lowell. Then I heard her repeat, "Boys don't baby-sit? Well, Logan does, but anyway, let me see. You know what, Mrs. Lowell? I *might* be able to sit after all. That is, if I'm not sitting for Emily Michelle. Did I tell you I have an adopted sister? She's Vietnamese. . . . What? You don't? . . . Yeah, well, I had a feeling. Later, Mrs. Lowell." Kristy hung up the phone. "We just lost a sitting job," she said.

"Good," I replied.

"She heard about Logan and Emily and suddenly — like magic — she didn't need a sitter anymore."

"What's wrong with *Logan*?" asked Mary Anne.

"He's a boy," said Kristy. "In Mrs. Lowell's world boys don't baby-sit. And *I* committed the crime of being a member of a family who adopted a Vietnamese child." Kristy's grin hadn't faded yet. "Hey, Dawn, Stacey, you blonde-haired, blue-eyed people — I bet you guys wouldn't have been good enough for Mrs. Lowell, either."

We were all starting to smile by then. "Why not?" asked Stacey.

"Because your parents are . . ." — Kristy dropped her voice to a whisper — ". . . *divorced*."

"Ooh!" I cried. "I'm telling! I'm telling Mrs. Lowell."

"You know what?" said Mary Anne. "When you think about it, none of us would be good enough for the Lowells. Claud, you're Japanese. Jessi, you're African-American. Stacey, Dawn, and Kristy, your parents are divorced. *I* have a stepsister. Oh, and by the way, I made the mistake of mentioning that to the Lowell kids. And Mallory — "

"Yeah?"

"Your family is just too darn big. Caitlin thinks you're Catholic. You know what else?" Mary Anne went on. "I feel sort of sorry for Mrs. Lowell."

"How sorry?" I asked.

Mary Anne held her thumb an eighth of an

inch from her finger. "This sorry," she said, giggling.

Later that evening I was sitting in the kitchen with my father. He was making salad dressing. I was chopping vegetables. "Dad?" I said. "Did anybody ever hate you because you're Japanese?"

Dad's back had been facing me. Now he turned away from the counter. "Why do you ask that, honey?"

"I was just wondering."

"Did something happen?"

"There's this woman named Mrs. Lowell. She's a baby-sitting client. She doesn't want me to sit for her kids because I'm Asian. That's never happened to me before. I mean, I don't understand. What's wrong with being Japanese?"

"Nothing," Dad answered. "And I'm sorry anyone made you feel you had to ask that question."

"Did you know," said Janine, who apparently had been listening to our conversation from somewhere nearby, "that during World War Two thousands of Japanese were interned in concentration camps in the United States?"

"In the United States?" I repeated, aghast. "There were concentration camps here in America?" My voice had grown shrill. "I thought the only concentration camps were the ones in Europe with those funny names. Treblinka and Dachau and — well, I don't remember any others, but we learned about them in school this year. Our teacher didn't tell us about death camps *here*, though, for Japanese people."

"They weren't death camps," said Janine. "But they were places where American Japanese were made to stay during the war."

"Because Japan and the U.S. were fighting on opposite sides?" I asked.

Janine nodded. "So Japanese-Americans weren't trusted, and they were pulled out of their homes, away from their jobs and lives, and made to stay locked up in camps."

"But they hadn't done anything wrong," I protested. And then I remembered what Mary Anne had said: Prejudice isn't rational. "How come people like Mrs. Lowell can't look underneath other people's skin? How come what's on the outside matters so much?" I asked.

"I don't know," Dad replied. "But I guess what's really important is that *you* can look underneath." My father smiled sadly at me.

CHAPTER 11

One Saturday, not long after Jackie had suggested putting on a show, we held a band rehearsal and nearly everyone came. All of us BSC members were there, and the kids just kept trickling into the Newtons' yard, clutching their instruments.

The Papadakis kids arrived with Karen, Andrew, and David Michael. Most of the kids from the neighborhood had shown up, as well as the younger brothers and sisters of the BSC members. I was standing in a noisy, happy crowd.

"Should we start the rehearseal now?" I asked Kristy.

"Let's wait a few more minutes," she answered. "If we do, maybe everybody will show up."

So we waited. Karen and her friends Nancy Dawes and Hannie Papadakis made up a dance to the "Little Girls" song. Then they surrounded Nicky Pike, hands on hips, singing, "Little girls! Little girls!" Nicky broke out of their circle and ran to David Michael. "Save me!" he cried.

The drum players — and there were quite a few of them — grouped together near the swing set, beating away happily.

Marilyn and Shea sat at the keyboard and played a duet.

"Claudia?" said Jackie, tapping my arm. "Can I make an announcement?"

"We're waiting for a few more kids to arrive," I told him.

"But I can't wait."

"He might as well go ahead," Dawn whispered to me. "I think the only kids who aren't here now are the Lowells."

I nodded. "Okay, Jackie. What's your announcement?"

"Shea, help me," said Jackie. "Help me get their attention."

Shea crashed out a chord on the keyboard. The kids gathered around him.

Jackie stood on an overturned plastic crate. "Everybody!" he said loudly. "I have an idea."

"Another one?" asked Vanessa Pike.

"Yup. It's about our show. I think we should play the songs from *Fiddler on the Roof*, not *Annie*."

"What's *Fiddler on the Roof*?" asked Becca Ramsey.

"I know!" cried Linny Papadakis. "We saw that show in Stamford."

It turned out that a lot of kids had. And many of them owned the music and were familiar with the songs. Still, not every kid knew what Jackie was talking about, so I said to him, "Tell them the story of *Fiddler on the Roof*."

"Okay," answered Jackie, pleased to have been trusted with that task. "See, there's this family with all these girls — "

"More *girls*?" protested Nicky.

" — living in Russia a long time ago," Jackie continued. "And their father wants them to get married, only he wants this lady called a matchmaker to choose husbands for them. But the daughters fall in love with other men. Also, a war is coming, and the family is in trouble because they're Jewish . . ." Jackie trailed off and glanced over his shoulder at me. "I'm not sure why that got them in trouble. I mean, why the soldiers didn't like them. Well, anyway." Jackie turned back to the kids. "And the soldiers want to make the family — and all the Jewish people in town — leave the place where they've been living. It's called Anatevka. And they have to pack up their stuff and find another home and it's very sad. But the songs are good and Shea knows how to play some of them and I think our program should be called *Fiddler on the Roof* instead of *Annie*," Jackie finished up.

The kids who had seen *Fiddler on the Roof*, which was more than half of them, agreed. Our entire program had changed.

"Shea? What song do you and Jackie want to teach the kids first?" I asked.

Shea considered this. "How about 'Tradition'? I like that one. It has a good beat. And we know most of the words."

"Okay. Let's start."

Soon after we began, the Lowell kids showed up. Mrs. Lowell was with them.

"Tradishu-u-u-u-un! Tra*d*ition!" the singers were belting out.

I glanced at Mrs. Lowell, then down at the ground. "Hi," I said. I wondered what she saw when she looked at me. Slope-eyes? That was why I couldn't look at *her*.

"Hello," replied Mrs. Lowell. She was gazing around the yard at the kids, who'd stopped playing and singing. Then she approached Dawn.

Caitlin, Mackie, and Celeste ran to the children.

"Are you one of the baby-sitters?" Mrs. Lowell asked Dawn. (She ignored the rest of us. You'd never have known that Mary Anne and Kristy and I had taken care of her kids.)

"Yes," Dawn answered warily.

"Are you in charge here?"

"Actually," said Dawn, straightening her shoulders, "Claudia is in charge. The band was her idea."

"Oh." Mrs. Lowell looked at me, then back at Dawn. She cleared her throat. "There certainly is an assortment of children here."

"Oh, yeah," said Dawn. "All ages. The youngest one is — " Dawn stopped speaking. She realized that wasn't what Mrs. Lowell had meant. She also realized Mrs. Lowell was right. The children *were* "assorted." Becca is African-American. Linny and Hannie are Greek. Nancy Dawes is Jewish, but Dawn didn't see how Mrs. Lowell could tell *that* just by looking at her. The Hsu boys are Asian. And did Mrs. Lowell know that the Rodowskys are Polish? Frankly, Dawn didn't care. "I guess," she said.

"What songs are the children learning?" asked Mrs. Lowell.

"They're learning music from *Fiddler on the Roof*. They just — "

"*Fiddler on the Roof*?" Mrs. Lowell's jaw tightened. Her lips were pressed together so firmly they were turning white. "Caitlin? Celeste? Mackie? Come here, please. We're going home."

"But Mom — " said Mackie.

"I mean it. Right this instant."

"We want to *play!*" wailed Celeste, banging her sticks together.

"You can play at home."

Mrs. Lowell meant business. Reluctantly her children made their way to her. Celeste's lower lip was trembling. As they pushed past me, Mrs. Lowell made a face. It was the sort of face you'd make if you opened up a package of meat and discovered it was moldy.

Stacey put her arm around me.

I wanted to cry, but I looked at the grinning members of All the Children. They didn't know what had happened and they were ready to play again. Shea started at the beginning of "Tradition" and worked slowly through the song while the children tried to memorize the melody.

"What was *that* all about?" Mary Anne whispered to me.

My friends and I stepped away and clustered together at the edge of the yard. Kristy was fuming. Her face was beet red.

"I guess they didn't like our choice of musicals," said Jessi.

"Because it's about Russian Jews?" asked Mal.

"That's a bad combination for Mrs. Lowell,"

I said. "Foreigners *and* people of a different religion." I attempted a smile. Kristy just shook her head.

"Hey, come on. You were the one who was able to laugh before," I said to her.

"I didn't have to face Mrs. Lowell then," Kristy answered. "I couldn't *see* how much she dislikes me because my sister is from Vietnam. It's a little different when you're actually looking at her."

"What do you think we should do now?" asked Stacey.

"What do you mean?" replied Dawn.

"About our program."

"Go ahead with it."

"What if other parents don't approve of the idea?"

"What other parents? None of them is like Mrs. Lowell. And half of them have already taken their kids to see *Fiddler on the Roof*. We can't change the program because Mrs. Lowell doesn't like it."

"I guess," said Stacey. "But you know what? When you get right down to it, we're just kids. We might be good baby-sitters — "

"We *are* good baby-sitters," interrupted Dawn.

" — but we're still just kids. And *these* kids, the ones in the band, are other people's children. Not ours. Their parents think they know what's best for them. So we have to go along with that."

Stacey was right. Who were we to think we could change the world?

"Wait a sec, you guys!" said Dawn. "You are worrying about a problem we don't even have. As I just said, the rest of the parents are nothing like Mrs. Lowell. As far as we know, they love the band and they love the songs their children are playing. So Caitlin and Celeste and Mackie can't be part of the band anymore. That's too bad. It really is. But there are a couple of dozen other kids" — Dawn spread her arms, indicating the crowd of children in the yard — "who still want to make music. Right?"

"Right," agreed Stacey. "Okay, Shea. Take it away!"

CHAPTER 12

My friends and I tried very hard to be cheerful after that, especially when we were around the kids. Still, I don't know about the other BSC members, but when I was alone, I brooded. Not so much about the music our band was playing. It didn't take me long to realize that not *too* many people would find fault with performing music from a show as long-running and as popular as *Fiddler on the Roof*. No, I brooded about my awful revelation. (By the way, Janine was the one who told me about *revelations*. She says a revelation is like a discovery, only more dramatic.)

The thing is, I'd never thought of myself as different until I met Mrs. Lowell. I mean, everyone is unique. There is no other Claudia Lynn Kishi, no one who looks just like me, and loves art and junk food and is poor at school but good with kids, and so forth. I learned *that* when I was little enough to watch

Sesame Street. What I hadn't learned is that there are people — in my very own neighborhood — who don't value me or find me worthwhile, just because my ancestors happen to have come from a particular country.

Plus, the Lowells and my revelation were so tied up with the band that for awhile the band left a bad taste in my mouth. I didn't enjoy it anymore. I didn't look forward to rehearsals.

But Karen Brewer changed that.

One Saturday afternoon I went to Kristy's house to baby-sit for her little brothers and sisters — David Michael, Emily Michelle, Andrew, and Karen. As usual, the rest of Kristy's family had scattered. Her mother and Watson had gone off for an afternoon of peace. Nannie was at a meeting. Kristy was with Mary Anne at the library, working on a school project. Sam was at the high school for a dress rehearsal of the drama club's latest play (he had helped write the play). And Charlie had gone off in his car, the Junk Bucket. I wasn't sure where, but it didn't matter. (In case of an emergency I had decided to call my own parents. They're usually pretty easy to find.)

"Well," Karen said to me as soon as Charlie and the Junk Bucket had driven off. "That's the last of them."

"Last of who?" I was sitting on the front steps of Kristy's house. Andrew, Emily, and

David Michael were fooling around in the yard. But Karen had plopped down next to me.

"The last of the big people," replied Karen. "Now it's just us little guys and you. The fun can begin."

I smiled. "What do you feel like doing today?"

"Playing."

"Playing what?" I was thinking I could tolerate anything except hide-and-seek, which I had played all afternoon the day before with the three Barrett kids. I was all seeked out. All hidden out, too.

"Our songs," said Karen. "Let's rehearse. Hannie and Nancy could come over. And maybe Linny."

"Well . . . how about playing hide-and-seek?" I said, which just goes to show how I was feeling about the band that day.

"No!" cried Karen. "We *need* to rehearse. Please? I'll even let Emily play with us. I'll give her a pot and a spoon. She can pretend she's another drummer. That way she won't feel left out."

How could I argue with that? Before I knew it, Nancy and Hannie and Linny had come over and the kids were performing "Miracle of Miracles." The tune came from Karen who was playing her kazoo, and Hannie, playing her harmonica. The other kids were playing cymbals, sticks, oatmeal drums, and the pot and spoon.

When the children had run through the song one time, Karen said, "Let's pretend we have a big audience. Here. Claudia, you sit on the grass and be the big audience. We will play on the steps. The steps are our stage."

The kids arranged themselves on the steps. Then Karen came forward. "Welcome, ladies and — I mean, welcome lady. I'm very, very glad you could come to our show. My name is, um, Lucretia Marissa von Brewer and this is my band. I am your emcee this evening. Tonight, for your listening pleasure — "

"Excuse me!" spoke up David Michael. "Excuse me, Miss von Brewer. How come you get to lead things, like always?"

"Because this was my idea," Karen replied. "Now, as I was saying, tonight we will favor you with that ever-popular song 'Anatevka.' " Karen turned back to her band. "Places, everyone! . . . Emily, I said, places! That means you. Hey, are you in this band or not?"

"Are you in this band or not?" Emily repeated. She was wandering around the yard, filling her pot with sticks and fallen leaves and flower petals.

"Claudia!" Karen complained to me.

"Why don't you go ahead and play without her . . . Miss von Brewer?"

"Okay. Ready, guys?" said Karen to her band. "And a-one and a-two!" "Anatevka" rang across the yard, accompanied by exuberant drumming. When the song was over, Karen took charge again. "Not bad," she said. "Not bad." She frowned. "Well, not great." She eyed the group on the steps. "You know what we need?" she said.

Hannie and Nancy perked up. "What?"

"Uniforms! I bet we would play better with band uniforms."

I smiled. I thought of the movie *The Music Man*, about this traveling salesman guy who calls himself Professor Harold Hill (he's really a con artist) and breezes into this little town, River City, Iowa, and convinces the parents there that a band is just what their kids need. He gets everyone to buy these expensive instruments and fancy uniforms from him, so the band looks really terrific. But Professor Hill never bothers to tell anyone that he's not a musician, he can't play a note, and he can't teach the kids to *play* their instruments. It doesn't matter. The kids gain self-confidence from the way they look and everything, so in the end they can play after all (or something like that).

I could understand why Karen wanted uniforms for our band.

"Hey, yeah! Uniforms!" cried David Michael

unexpectedly. (He is not generally a fan of Karen's ideas.) "That would be way cool, right, Linny?"

"Yeah!"

"Okay," said Karen. "Then I will take charge. Allow me."

"You're in charge *again*?" cried Andrew.

"I have *lots* of ideas," said Karen haughtily. "Come on, Nancy. Come on, Hannie. I want you guys to help me."

Karen and her friends disappeared into the house. While we waited for them, Linny said, gazing into space, "I think blue uniforms would be good. With stripes up each leg. And blue hats."

"We'd look like policemen," protested David Michael.

"I think we should wear boots and spurs and chaps and ten-gallon hats and carry lassos," said Andrew.

"We want *u*niforms, not *co*stumes," David Michael replied.

"Oh. Well, what do band uniforms look like?"

The front door to the house burst open then. "They look like *this*!" cried Karen. She and Hannie and Nancy tiptoed between the boys and pranced onto the lawn.

I bit my lip to keep from laughing.

The girls were wearing long slips, clumpy

106

high-heeled shoes, and feather boas. Plus, Karen was wearing a straw hat, Hannie was wearing a motorcycle helmet, and Nancy was wearing a bride's veil.

"Dress ups!" cried Emily Michelle. She dropped her pot and ran to Karen. "I dress up! I dress up!"

David Michael, Linny, and Andrew stood on the steps, their mouths open. They couldn't speak. They could only stare.

"How do we look?" Karen asked me.

"You look . . . beautiful."

"Yeah, to Frankenstein," said Linny, recovering the power of speech.

"Do you really think those are *band* uniforms?" David Michael managed to ask. "Andrew's idea was better than this. He wanted everyone to dress as cowboys."

"What's wrong with these outfits?" asked Karen.

"You expect *boys* to wear slips and high heels?" answered Linny.

"No. I guess not. . . . But we couldn't find band uniforms," admitted Karen.

"Hey, I know!" exclaimed Nancy. "How about if all the band members just dress the same? We could wear, like, jeans and red shirts. I bet everyone has a pair of jeans and a red shirt."

David Michael opened his mouth, then

closed it. Apparently he could find nothing wrong with the idea.

"I have jeans!" exclaimed Andrew. "And a red sweat shirt."

"I have jeans and a red blouse," said Hannie.

"I have jeans and a red T-shirt," said Nancy. "The T-shirt says *'My parents went to Hawaii and all they brought me was this dumb shirt.'* "

We laughed. And Linny added, "Hey, maybe we could have red T-shirts made that say ALL THE CHILDREN on them. Then we would really look alike."

Even David Michael liked that idea.

"Well," I said, "I'll find out how much the shirts would cost. Maybe we could raise money to buy them."

"Or we could ask for donations at our first band concert," said Karen.

"You guys had better be *really* good then," I said.

"Don't worry. We will. Come on, let's rehearse, everybody!"

And the kids played "Anatevka" with new enthusiasm.

For awhile that afternoon I forgot about the Lowells.

CHAPTER 13

─── MEET ───
ALL THE CHILDREN
Come to our first band concert!

ENJOY THE MUSIC FROM
Fiddler on the Roof!

PLACE: The Newtons' backyard
DAY: Saturday the 6th
TIME: 2:00 p.m.
ADMISSION: Free — everyone is welcome!

───────── ★ ─────────
DONATIONS ACCEPTED:
WE NEED BAND UNIFORMS!
───────── ★ ─────────

"How are we doing?" I asked.

"One more stack," Jessi replied. "And it's a short one."

"Did we get rid of the fliers with those misspelled words?" Kristy wanted to know.

"*Yes*," I answered testily. The misspelled words had been my fault, of course. The first few fliers I had lettered had said things like "the Newtons bake yerd," and "every one is welcomh!" and "WE NEED BAD UNIFORMS!" Then Kristy had leaned over my shoulder and realized what I was doing. She'd given me a new job: decorating each flier. So what if I can't spell? Drawing little instruments and designs on the fliers was much more fun than lettering them.

It was a Friday evening. I had invited my friends to stay after our meeting and eat a pizza supper. Now we were sprawled around my room, preparing for the first band concert. It was going to be held in a week. We needed time to distribute our fliers. We were hoping lots of people would be free on Saturday at 2:00. Our kids were looking forward to a big audience.

My friends and I planned to post the fliers the next day and to hand them out to our neighbors. But we wanted the kids to be involved with inviting guests, too, so at our next rehearsal we were going to hand each band member one invitation to give to someone special.

"Boy, I hope the kids are going to be ready for the concert," said Dawn.

"Oh, they will be," I assured her. "The ones who play the important instruments — not that the sticks and the oatmeal drums aren't important, but you know what I mean — the kids on the keyboard and the guitar and stuff have already learned the music. And the others follow along *well*. I think the concert is going to be great."

"So what's our schedule this week?" asked Stacey.

"Short rehearsals on Monday, Tuesday, and Wednesday," I replied, "dress rehearsals — or whatever they're called — on Thursday and Friday, and the performance on Saturday."

"I hope everyone can fit into the Newtons' yard," said Mary Anne.

"Oh, don't worry about that," I replied.

Mary Anne smiled. "What *should* I worry about?"

"Oh, things like whether Jackie will knock over the keyboard while Shea and Marilyn are playing it — "

"Or whether Claire will have a tantrum if she makes a mistake," said Mal.

"Or whether Karen will decide to perform

in her bathing suit or something," said Kristy. "You know, she likes our band uniforms, and she especially likes the idea of getting T-shirts, but she still wants to perform in an outfit that's a little, oh, flashier."

"Her *bath*ing suit?" I said.

"Well, you know, for instance, in her bathing suit with a crown and high heels so she could be Miss Kazoo."

"Oh, my lord. Miss Kazoo," I repeated, but I was giggling.

Six days later, on Thursday afternoon, not long after school had let out, the first dress rehearsal of All the Children got underway.

Everyone was nervous.

"Do you realize," began Stacey, edging closer to me, "that this time Saturday the concert will be over?"

"I wonder if everybody will be in one piece," said Dawn, who had overheard.

"We can only hope," I replied.

"At least," said Kristy, "the kids remembered to bring their instruments *and* wear their uniforms. That's a good sign."

She was right. It was a good sign. Then again, I thought I had once heard Janine say something like, "Good dress rehearsal, bad opening night." Maybe we didn't want the dress rehearsals to go too well after all. Not if that would jinx the concert.

I watched the kids enter the yard. Some filed in alone. Most arrived in pairs or in groups of three or four. All were wearing blue jeans with sneakers and red tops.

When everyone had arrived, Kristy tapped my shoulder. "Okay, Claud," she said. "Let's get started."

I clapped my hands and the kids gathered around me. "This is a dress rehearsal," I reminded the kids. "Remember what that means? It means we play every song, and we put on the program just the way we're going to put it on when we have an audience. We don't stop for mistakes because we won't be able to do that on Saturday. We keep on going no matter what. So now — you guys pretend that Stacey and Jessi and Kristy and Mal and Mary Anne and Dawn and I are your audience. In fact, we are your audience. And it's two o'clock on Saturday afternoon. Everyone has arrived and they're sitting patiently, waiting for the concert to begin. Jackie? Are you ready?"

Jackie stepped forward. Then he turned around and scrutinized the band. The children had arranged themselves as we had practiced — the kids playing "real" instruments in front, the kids playing kazoos and percussion grouped behind them, and the singers standing in a semicircle at one side. Jackie nodded to them. Then he faced his audience again.

"Welcome, parents and friends," he said loudly. He paused thoughtfully, then added, "And brothers and sisters and grandparents." Another pause. "Oh, and stepbrothers and . . . and, well, and stepfamilies." (He was covering all bases.) "And teachers . . ." (At this point I almost whispered, "Enough, Jackie!" but he was on his own.) "And aunts and uncles and cousins. Um, welcome," he said again. "Today I am proud to present All the Children. This is our new band and this is our first concert. We are playing music from . . . from . . ."

"From *Fiddler on the Roof*!" hissed Karen.

"I know *that*!" Jackie hissed back. "From that ever-popular musical, which my brothers and I have actually seen in Stamford, *Fiddler on the Roof*. And now for our first song, 'Anatevka.' " Jackie pointed to Shea and Marilyn. "Hit it, boys!" he called, and Marilyn flashed him an angry look. "I mean, um, hit it, kids!"

Jackie ran to the kazoo players, tripped over his untied shoelaces, fell over Mathew Hobart, the violin player, and lost his kazoo.

I closed my eyes briefly.

When I opened them again, the children had

sorted themselves out and Jackie had located his kazoo. At the keyboard, Shea and Marilyn glanced at each other. Then Shea nodded and the first chords of "Anatevka" danced across the lawn. One by one, the other kids joined in and soon everyone was singing or playing.

When the song ended, the members of the BSC clapped loudly.

All the Children performed two more songs.

During the fourth number, "Tradition," Claire lost her place. In a rest (that was supposed to be silent, of course) she banged on her oatmeal drum. Then she clapped her hand over her mouth.

"Uh-oh!" said Suzy Barrett loudly. "You did a boo-boo."

"I know it," replied Claire. Around her the music was starting up. But Claire's temper had taken over. "Quiet!" she yelled. "Quiet! . . . I said *quiet*! We have to go back!"

"Claire did a boo-boo," Suzy said again.

The band was confused. Some kids continued to play, others had stopped, several had lost their places.

"What should I do?" I whispered to Kristy.

"See if they can fix it themselves," she replied.

"If they can't, I'll take Claire aside," added Mal. "Maybe I should be prepared to do that on Saturday, too."

The band was nearly out of control when Jackie yelled, "START OVER! AND A-ONE AND A-TWO!"

Claire pouted for one entire verse, then joined in again.

"Whew," I said under my breath.

After one more song, Jackie announced, "And now it is time for a station break. . . . I mean, for intermission." He glanced at me, then added, "By the way, the band is trying to buy cool red T-shirts for our uniforms. If you would like to help us, we'd be glad to take your money. Remember — this concert is free. You did not have to pay to get into the Newtons' yard."

The kids relaxed for several moments, and I called Jackie over. Before I had opened my mouth he said, "I know we didn't rehearse that last part. It's new. I wrote it myself last night."

"And you did a good job," I told him, trying to be tactful, "but I don't think you need to say that. On Saturday we'll leave out baskets for donations. Please don't remind the audience that they didn't pay to see the show. I'm not sure they'll appreciate that."

"Okay, okay."

Jackie walked away and I stifled a laugh. I noticed Jessi and Stacey doing the same thing. Across the lawn, Mallory was having a talk with Claire. When Mal joined us again, Jackie shouted, "Okay, everybody! That's the end of intermission. You can sit down now!"

"Is that how he's going to talk to the *audience* on Saturday?" said Mary Anne, sounding horrified.

"Maybe the grown-ups will think it's funny," whispered Jessi.

"Maybe. But I have a feeling I better talk to him before tomorrow's rehearsal. I don't want anyone to be offended," I said.

When the dress rehearsal ended I had another chat with Jackie. I tried to explain the meaning of the word *tact*. I'm not sure I did a very good job. "Be polite, Jackie," I said finally.

"Polite," he repeated seriously.

"Say things you'd like to hear if you were in the audience. Make the audience feel good. Flatter them."

"Flatter them."

"Just use good sense."

"Claudia?"

"Yeah?"

"I think maybe I was born without good sense."

CHAPTER 14

The time: 5:05 p.m.

The day: Friday.

Twenty-four hours from that moment the first public performance of All the Children would be over. I wasn't even going to be *in* the performance and I was nervous. I kept remembering Claire's temper tantrum and Jackie's guilt trip, which he hoped would bring in money for T-shirts.

"Oh, my lord," I muttered.

"What's the matter?"

I whirled around. "Geez, Kristy, don't sneak up on me!"

"I didn't sneak up on you," she replied indignantly. "I ran up the stairs like I always do. And I am not a quiet person."

"I know."

"Thanks a lot."

"Well, you said it." Kristy made a face at

me. "Oh, I'm sorry," I told her. "I'm nervous about the concert. I didn't mean to take it out on you."

"The rehearsal went really well today," said Kristy, flopping onto my bed. "You don't have to worry."

"Well, I'm worrying anyway. A little bit. I've been thinking about Claire's tantrum and Jackie's speech."

"But Claire didn't have a tantrum today. And Jackie's speech was much better than yesterday's. Shorter, too."

"You're right."

"Come on. Leave the worrying to Mary Anne. She's a professional worrier."

"I heard that!" exclaimed Mary Anne as she entered my room.

"Now *you're* sneaking around!" I accused her.

"What?" said Mary Anne. "And Kristy, I do *not* worry professionally."

Jessi ran into the room then, grinning. "I wish you guys could hear yourselves," she said. "My mother would say you are sniping and griping."

"Has anyone ever heard that saying about 'good dress rehearsal, bad opening night'?" I asked my friends.

"I have," Jessi answered.

"Do you believe it?"

Jessi shrugged. "I don't know. It's a superstition."

"Anyway, we can't do much about tomorrow now," said Kristy. "We've held millions of rehearsals. I think the kids are as good as they're going to get. We'll just hope for the best."

The rest of the members of the BSC trickled in, and by five-thirty Kristy was ready to begin the meeting.

"Any club business?" she asked after she'd called us to order.

"Yeah," I replied. "The Lowells."

Six heads turned slowly toward me. "The Lowells," Jessi repeated.

"I guess we could consider them unfinished business," said Kristy. "We haven't talked about them in awhile. Claud's right. We need to."

"Why?" asked Stacey, sounding whiny.

"What are you complaining about, O Blonde-Haired, Blue-Eyed One?" I asked. "They didn't say *you* were funny-looking."

"Exactly. How do you think I feel — being approved of by Mrs. Lowell? I don't want *her* approval. It's like, if *she* approves of me, then what's wrong with me? Something must be. See what I mean?"

"I understand," said Dawn, "but how come

you let Mrs. Lowell affect how you feel about yourself?"

Stacey paused. "I don't know," she said.

"Anyway, that isn't the point," said Kristy. "The point is — what if Mrs. Lowell calls the club again, wanting another sitter?"

"Do you really think she's going to?" asked Stacey.

Kristy shrugged. "Who knows? She might."

"Or what if the kids show up at a band rehearsal one day? That could happen, too," I said.

"Well, I think we need to teach the Lowells a lesson," Mal spoke up.

"How?" asked Dawn.

"I'm not sure. But I want to get back at them for the way they treated Claudia and Jessi. That was rude and mean and . . . and, well, dumb."

"How are we going to teach Mrs. Lowell a lesson?" asked Kristy. "We're just a bunch of kids."

"The next time she calls we should tell her we're not going to sit for her family anymore because we don't like bigots," I said hotly.

"Claudia. You know darn well we cannot say that," Kristy replied.

"Okay, we'll say we don't sit for blonde-haired, blue-eyed people."

"Claudia! Geez!" cried Dawn. "Stace and I

are blonde-haired, blue-eyed people. Besides, if we say anything like that then we're no better than the Lowells. That's bigoted, too."

"Isn't there a term for that?" said Stacey. "Reverse something-or-other?"

"Oh, who cares," I said.

"You know, we really ought to teach Caitlin and Mackie and Celeste a lesson," said Mal. "But not a mean one; just that most people are nice. If we don't do that and they grow up prejudiced, it'll be our fault."

"No, it won't," interrupted Jessi. "It'll be their parents' fault. It's already their parents' fault."

Ring, ring.

I dove for the phone. A split second before I picked it up, I remembered not to sound angry. I drew in a deep breath. "Hello, Baby-sitters Club."

"Hi . . . Claudee?"

"Hi, Jamie!" I said brightly. (Not too many people call me Claudee.)

"Hi-hi. Um, Mommy said I could telephone you. I was worrying about something. What if it rains tomorrow?"

I opened my eyes wide. Then I covered the mouthpiece of the phone and said to my friends, "Oh, my lord! What if it rains tomorrow? We never thought about that. The electric keyboard can't be on the porch if it rains. The rain always blows in. This is a disaster!"

"Claud," said Kristy calmly, "it isn't a disaster yet. It isn't raining. And the weatherman is predicting sunshine for tomorrow."

"Well, what does he know?"

"If it rains, we'll figure something out. We'll set up the band in the garage so the kids won't get wet."

"But the audience can't fit in the garage, too."

Then we'll cancel," hissed Kristy. She waved wildly at the phone. "Talk to Jamie before he hangs up."

"Jamie?" I said sweetly. "Don't worry about it. See you tomorrow."

I hung up the phone.

"The Lowells — " Jessi began to say.

Ring, ring.

"I'll get it this time," said Kristy, eyeing me. "Hello, Baby-sitters Club." Pause. "Karen? What's the matter? . . . Your kazoo? Well, did you look *every*where in your room? . . . Okay, how about the car? . . . Are you sure you had it when you left rehearsal this afternoon? . . . What? You blasted it in Andrew's ear on the way home?" Kristy tried not to giggle. "Well, maybe Andrew has it. Maybe he doesn't want to be blasted at anymore. . . . Okay, put Andrew on. . . . Hi, Andrew. Listen, you don't know where Karen's kazoo is, do you? You know, she *needs* it for the concert. And if she can't find hers, then I'll lend her Sam's. . . . You just remembered where it is? Okay, why don't you go find it, and give the phone back to Karen." Kristy paused again and made a face. For a moment she held the phone away from her ear. Then she said, "Karen, what on earth is going on? . . . No, let Andrew get the kazoo himself. You don't have to see his hiding place."

Kristy stayed on the phone for over five minutes, straightening out the problems between Andrew and Karen. By the time she hung up, Andrew had produced the missing kazoo and Karen had apologized for nearly deafening him earlier. Kristy was laughing, but she quickly became sober. "Okay. The Lowells," she said to us. "We haven't made a decision yet."

"I have an idea," said Jessi. "I think if Mrs. Lowell calls the BSC again we should just tell her that no one can take the job. If that happens a few times, she'll stop calling."

"I guess," I replied with a sigh. "But then nobody has learned anything, except us. And we didn't need the lessons we learned."

"Maybe teaching the Lowells a lesson isn't our job," said Dawn.

"You know we *can* do one thing," said Jessi.

"What?" (The rest of us practically pounced on her.)

"We can be good examples for the kids we sit for. For *all* of them, whether they have prejudiced ideas or not."

"Yeah!" exclaimed Stacey. Then she added more seriously. "But we don't want to impose our ideas on them."

"No," agreed Jessi. "We can just show them how to be good neighbors."

Everyone was silent for a few moments. Then I said, "You know what? This may be hard to believe, but I can't hate the Lowells. I feel as though I *ought* to hate them, but I just can't."

"My parents," spoke up Mal, "say it's okay to hate some of the things people *do*, but it's not okay to hate the people who do them."

"Like Karen hating the fact that Andrew hid her kazoo, but not hating Andrew," said Kristy.

I frowned. "You guys? This is too much like school. Let's have a junk-food fest or something."

Mary Anne looked at her watch. "Too late. It's almost six. We don't have time. Anyway, let's be good girls and not spoil our appetites for dinner."

"But *we're* having liver," I objected.

"Then by all means scarf up a candy bar before you go downstairs," said Mallory. "Liver. Ew. Why not just serve up monkey or something?"

"Monkey!" exclaimed Kristy. "Hey — "

"Oh, please don't start," wailed Mary Anne. "Mal, why did you mention disgusting food? That's Kristy's favorite subject."

Kristy ignored her. "Six o'clock," she announced. "Meeting adjourned."

"Wait!" I cried. "Don't leave yet. The concert starts at two. Meet here at one o'clock tomorrow. Wear jeans and red shirts like the kids. Who's bringing those baskets for donations?"

"I am," said Mallory. "I found three."

"And who's bringing chairs?" (We had decided to provide a few folding chairs for older people in the audience. Everyone else would have to sit on the ground, like at any outdoor concert.)

"Me!" said Mary Anne, Dawn, Jessi, and Stacey.

Kristy looked at me. "Is that it, Claud?"

"I think so."

"Okay. See you guys tomorrow."

"And keep your fingers crossed for sunshine!" I added.

CHAPTER 15

I had nightmares about rain and thunderstorms. In one, All the Children were performing in Jamie's yard on a sunny, perfect day. Then, without warning, a storm blew in. It blew in so quickly that the children and the audience couldn't even run for cover before a bolt of lightning sliced down through the porch roof and struck the keyboard. The keyboard lit up like a neon sign, then crumbled into a little pile of ashes. Shea and Marilyn stood over it, their hands still poised to play, their mouths forming round O's of surprise.

In the dream, I screamed. (I hope I didn't *really* scream. That would be too, too embarrassing.) And then the storm blew away, and the concert began again, and Shea and Marilyn played air guitar instead of the keyboard. The audience thought the lightning had been a special effect, and they applauded loudly at

127

the end of the concert and donated enough money for all the red T-shirts we needed.

Maybe that wasn't a nightmare after all.

At any rate, I was relieved to wake up on Saturday and see that the sun was shining. (Frankly, I was relieved just to wake up.) The sky was a deep, clear blue, without so much as a hint of a cloud. Still, I jumped out of bed, ran to my phone, and dialed W-E-A-T-H-E-R.

"Good morning," said a tinny female voice. "Thank you for calling Weather. Here are today's readings and forecasts. Highs in the low seventies, lows tonight in the high fifties. The current temperature is a pleasant sixty-two degrees."

"Is it going to RAIN?" I shouted.

"Stay tuned for the remainder of the forecast following — "

I held the phone in front of me and said, "'What is this? The Telephone Company Variety Show?"

I listened for another minute and the weatherwoman assured me that the day would be "brilliantly sunny."

"Thank you," I said to her, and hung up.

That was at eight-fifteen. At one o'clock, when my friends began to arrive, the sun really was brilliant.

"Hey! What a great day!" called Kristy as she ran across the lawn.

I was sitting on the front stoop. "I know. We are *so* lucky."

Mallory showed up then with three wicker baskets, and soon the others arrived (in cars) with wooden and metal folding chairs, which their parents drove over to the Newtons'.

By one-thirty Jamie's yard looked like . . . well, it looked like a yard with a bunch of chairs in it.

Jamie dashed outside and tested every chair. "This one's good, this one's good," he kept saying.

Meanwhile, the members of the Baby-sitters Club ran an extension cord out of the Newtons' house and connected it to the keyboard. Someone set up three small tables and Mallory placed a basket on each one.

I propped up a sign by the garage. I had lettered it myself (but Stacey had given me a hand with the spelling). The sign said:

ALL THE CHILDREN
PREMIERE PERFORMANCE . . .
HERE . . . TODAY!
EVERYONE WELCOME
ADMISSION FREE
(DONATIONS ACCEPTED)

"We're here! We're here!" cried a small voice.

I looked away from the sign.

Running up Jamie's driveway, dressed in jeans and their red T-shirts, were Gabbie and Myriah Perkins.

"Are you ready?" I asked them, smiling.

"Very ready," said Gabbie seriously.

The members of All the Children began to arrive quickly after that. The ones who lived nearby walked to Jamie's on their own. Others showed up accompanied by their parents, and we had to separate the moms and dads from their kids so we could organize the band.

"Where's Jackie?" I asked at ten minutes to two. "We need our emcee. What are we going to do if he doesn't show up?"

"Claud!" exclaimed Kristy, exasperated. "You sound like Mary Anne again."

"And I heard that again," said Mary Anne. "Listen, you guys should be glad to have me around. I will personally do all your worrying for you. Claudia, you're not taking full advantage of me."

"Hello, everybody!" called a familiar voice.

"Jackie!" I replied, before I had even turned around. Then I ran to him and hugged him. "Oh, I'm *so* glad you're here!"

Jackie pulled away from me, pink-faced. "Do *not* hug me," he hissed. "You are a *girl*!" He searched the faces in the yard. "I hope Nicky didn't see that," he added nervously.

I grinned. "Oh, Jackie. Come on, let's get organized. The show will start in ten minutes. And look how big our audience is."

Jackie Rodowsky stood in front of the company of All the Children, who were arranged behind him in neat blue-jeaned, red-shirted groups. In front of him were grandparents and parents and children and neighbors and friends. Most of them were seated comfortably on blankets or beach towels. The others occupied the folding chairs.

The audience looked expectantly at Jackie as he said, "Welcome, Lysol and germs. You know, a funny thing happened to me on my way over to this backyard." Jackie glanced questioningly at me, and I waved my arms back and forth. I was sending him a gigantic NO signal.

(Next to me, Kristy had buried her head in her hands and was muttering, "I don't believe it. Who does he think he is? Johnny Carson?")

Luckily, Jackie got my message. He started over again. "Welcome, parents and friends, brothers and sisters, and grandparents and families," he said. (I heaved a sigh. Kristy unburied her face.) "Today I am proud to present All the Children. This is our new band and this is our first concert and actually this was all my idea."

"Jackie! Jackie!" called Claire Pike from the oatmeal drum section. "You aren't supposed to say that! You didn't say it before!"

Jackie ignored Claire. "We will be playing music from . . . from . . ."

"From *Fiddler on the Roof*!" supplied Karen, and several people laughed.

"From that ever-popular musical *Fiddler on the Roof*," said Jackie. "And now for our first song, 'Anatevka.' Hit it, Shea and Marilyn."

Jackie ran to the kazoo players (without tripping). He did drop his kazoo twice before getting a solid grip on it, but I don't think anyone noticed.

When "Anatevka" came to an end, the audience clapped. Kristy's big brothers even whistled. Then Shea and Marilyn played the opening notes of "If I Were a Rich Man." This was a difficult piece. We had arranged the number so that the keyboard and violin and guitar often played while the other instruments were at rest.

But Claire kept forgetting.

The third time she beat her drum out of turn, Archie nudged her.

The fourth time, Claire opened her mouth and —

"She's going to yell!" I whispered urgently to Mallory.

Mal looked calm. "I don't think so. I told

her that if she *had* to yell, she should do it inside her head."

Sure enough, Claire closed her mouth a few moments later.

The rest of the song, and the entire first portion of the concert, went quite well. Buddy Barrett sang once when everyone else was quiet, Charlotte forgot part of the music for "Tradition," and Jackie dropped his kazoo several more times, but nobody cared much.

Before the intermission, Jackie announced politely that there were three baskets for donations for the band T-shirts — but that was all he said. And when the concert ended he said, "Thank you for coming. I hope you enjoyed our show."

I wish someone had videotaped the concert. I really do. Especially the end. After Jackie thanked the audience, they clapped and clapped (and whistled) and clapped some more. Then a whole bunch of the parents stood up, ran to their kids, and hugged them and congratulated them.

"I'd say this was a success," I shouted to Stacey over the noise.

Stacey grinned. "Definitely!"

The yard seemed like a train station at rush hour; people running here and there, calling to one another. I looked from side to side, surveying the scene, and I saw two small figures sidling toward the gate in the Newtons' fence. Caitlin and Mackie Lowell.

Jessi was standing next to me and I elbowed her. "Look!" I exclaimed, pointing to the Lowell kids.

Jessi looked just in time to see them run through the gate and down the sidewalk toward their street. "I don't believe it," she murmured. "I bet their parents don't know they're here."

"Probably not. You know what? When I first noticed them they looked kind of sad." *Wistful* was the word I meant to use.

"I bet they wish they were playing today. I think they wanted to be in the concert," said Jessi.

"Even with *us* around? The funny-looking ones."

"I guess so."

"Jessi," I began thoughtfully, "do you think the Lowell kids *really* thought we were funny-looking or . . . or mean or stupid or whatever? Or were they just repeating things they heard their parents say?"

"I don't know."

"Because I was thinking. Right now Caitlin and Mackie and Celeste are pretty young. Maybe when they get older their opinions will change. Maybe they won't just automatically think what their parents think."

"You mean maybe they'll grow out of this?"

"It's possible. After all, they go to school. I don't know which school they go to, but there must be at least a *few* Asian kids and African-American kids and Jewish kids there."

"Yeah."

"And today they looked like they really wanted to be a part of this."

"Maybe we'll see them around the neighborhood sometimes."

"Maybe."

"Maybe one day they'll even be members of All the Children again."

"Maybe."

"Claudia! Claudia! How did I do?" cried Jackie, running to me.

I wanted to hug him, but instead I stood back and smiled. "Fantastic!"

"You should see the money everyone's giving us!"

"A lot?"

"Pretty much. . . . Did I really do a good job?"

"You really did."

"How good?"

I couldn't resist. I wrapped my arms around him in another hug. "Like I said, fantastic."

"Thank you," Jackie replied politely.

Dear Reader,

The idea for *Keep Out, Claudia!* was suggested to me by Olivia Ford, the daughter of a publishing colleague. Olivia's idea was for a book about prejudice and racism that centered around Claudia and the Kishis. Racism had been a topic in a number of Jessi's books, and Olivia felt that it would be realistic if one of the other characters in the series faced this problem, too.

The members of the Baby-sitters Club are a diverse group of kids. They come from different kinds of families, and from a variety of backgrounds. Each has her own interests and problems, yet the girls get along well as a group, and appreciate each other's differences. The kids they sit for are diverse, too. Their families come from various ethnic and religious backgrounds, and like the members of the BSC, the kids come from many different family situations. In addition, the baby-sitters take care of Rosie Wilder, who is highly gifted; Shea Rodowsky, who has learning disabilities; Matt Braddock, who is profoundly hearing impaired; and Susan Felder, who has autism.

As you can see, a recurring theme in the Baby-sitters Club books is that of tolerance and acceptance, rather than exclusion. It's something the characters feel strongly about, and so do I.

Happy reading,

Ann M. Martin

L. GODWIN

Ann M. Martin

About the Author

ANN MATTHEWS MARTIN was born on August 12, 1955. She grew up in Princeton, NJ, with her parents and her younger sister, Jane.

Although Ann used to be a teacher and then an editor of children's books, she's now a full-time writer. She gets the ideas for her books from many different places. Some are based on personal experiences. Others are based on childhood memories and feelings. Many are written about contemporary problems or events.

All of Ann's characters, even the members of the Baby-sitters Club, are made up. (So is Stoneybrook.) But many of her characters are based on real people. Sometimes Ann names her characters after people she knows, other times she chooses names she likes.

In addition to the Baby-sitters Club books, Ann Martin has written many other books for children. Her favorite is *Ten Kids, No Pets* because she loves big families and she loves animals. Her favorite Baby-sitters Club book is *Kristy's Big Day*. (By the way, Kristy is her favorite baby-sitter!)

Ann M. Martin now lives in New York with her cats, Gussie and Woody. Her hobbies are reading, sewing, and needlework — especially making clothes for children.

THE BABY-SITTERS CLUB

Notebook Pages

This Baby-sitters Club book belongs to ———————— .

I am ——————— years old and in the ———————

grade.

The name of my school is ———————————— .

I got this BSC book from ———————————— .

I started reading it on ———————————— and

finished reading it on ———————————— .

The place where I read most of this book is ——————— .

My favorite part was when ———————————— .

If I could change anything in the story, it might be the part when

———————————————————— .

My favorite character in the Baby-sitters Club is ——————— .

The BSC member I am most like is ————————————

because ————————————————————

If I could write a Baby-sitters Club book it would be about ———

————————————————————————

#56 Keep Out, Claudia!

The BSC members are shocked and saddened when they realize why Mrs. Lowell has asked that Claudia and Jessi not sit for her children. This is what I think about Mrs. Lowell and what she did: _____

_____

_____. If I were to come across someone like Mrs. Lowell, this is what I'd want to say to him/her: _____

_____

_____. The BSC members would like to teach the Lowell kids that prejudice and intolerance are wrong. Here are some ways to fight prejudice and intolerance: _____

_____

_____.

CLAUDIA'S

A spooky sitting adventure

Finger painting at 3...

Sitting for two of my favorite charges --
Jamie and Lucy Newton.

SCRAPBOOK

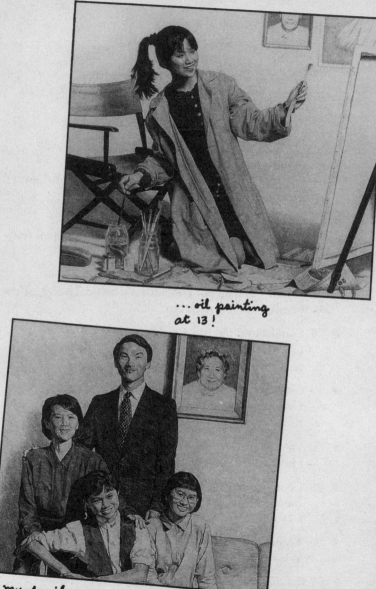

...oil painting at 13!

my family. Mom and Dad, me and Janine... and we'll never forget Mimi.

Interior art by Angelo Tillery

Read all the books
about **Claudia**
in the Baby-sitters Club series
by Ann M. Martin

\# 2 *Claudia and the Phantom Phone Calls*
Someone mysterious is calling Claudia!

\# 7 *Claudia and Mean Janine*
Claudia's big sister is super smart . . . and super
mean.

\# 12 *Claudia and the New Girl*
Claudia might give up the club — and it's all Ash-
ley's fault.

\# 19 *Claudia and the Bad Joke*
When Claudia baby-sits for a practical joker, she's
headed for big trouble.

\# 26 *Claudia and the Sad Good-bye*
Claudia never thought anything bad would happen to her grandmother, Mimi.

\# 33 *Claudia and the Great Search*
Claudia thinks she was adopted — and no one
told her about it.

\# 40 *Claudia and the Middle School Mystery*
How could anyone accuse *Claudia* of cheating?

\# 49 *Claudia and the Genius of Elm Street*
Baby-sitting for a seven-year-old genius makes
Claudia feel like a world-class dunce.

\# 56 *Keep Out, Claudia!*
Who wouldn't want Claudia for a baby-sitter?

\# 63 *Claudia's Friend Friend*
Claudia and Shea can't spell — but they can be
friends!

71 *Claudia and the Perfect Boy*
Love is in the air when Claudia starts a personals column in the school! paper.

78 *Claudia and Crazy Peaches*
Claudia's crazy Aunt Peaches is back in town. Let the games begin!

85 *Claudia Kishi, Live From WSTO!*
Claudia wins a contest to have her own radio show.

91 *Claudia and the First Thanksgiving*
Claudia's in the middle of a big Thanksgiving controversy!

97 *Claudia and the World's Cutest Baby*
Claudia can't take her eyes off of her adorable new niece.

#101 *Claudia Kishi, Middle School Dropout*
It's back to seventh grade for Claudia.

Mysteries:

6 *The Mystery at Claudia's House*
Claudia's room has been ransacked! Can the baby-sitters track down whodunnit?

11 *Claudia and the Mystery at the Museum*
Burglaries, forgeries . . . something crooked is going on at the new museum in Stoneybrook!

16 *Claudia and the Clue in the Photograph*
Has Claudia caught a thief — on film?

21 *Claudia and the Recipe for Danger*
There's nothing half-baked about the attempts to sabotage a big cooking contest!

Portrait Collection:

Claudia's Book
Claudia's design for living.

The Baby-Sitters Club®

Collect 'em all!

100 (and more) Reasons to Stay Friends Forever!

☐ MG43388-1	#1	Kristy's Great Idea	$3.50
☐ MG43387-3	#10	Logan Likes Mary Anne!	$3.99
☐ MG43717-8	#15	Little Miss Stoneybrook...and Dawn	$3.50
☐ MG43722-4	#20	Kristy and the Walking Disaster	$3.50
☐ MG43347-4	#25	Mary Anne and the Search for Tigger	$3.50
☐ MG42498-X	#30	Mary Anne and the Great Romance	$3.50
☐ MG42508-0	#35	Stacey and the Mystery of Stoneybrook	$3.50
☐ MG44082-9	#40	Claudia and the Middle School Mystery	$3.25
☐ MG43574-4	#45	Kristy and the Baby Parade	$3.50
☐ MG44969-9	#50	Dawn's Big Date	$3.50
☐ MG44968-0	#51	Stacey's Ex-Best Friend	$3.50
☐ MG44966-4	#52	Mary Anne + 2 Many Babies	$3.50
☐ MG44967-2	#53	Kristy for President	$3.25
☐ MG44965-6	#54	Mallory and the Dream Horse	$3.25
☐ MG44964-8	#55	Jessi's Gold Medal	$3.25
☐ MG45657-1	#56	Keep Out, Claudia!	$3.50
☐ MG45658-X	#57	Dawn Saves the Planet	$3.50
☐ MG45659-8	#58	Stacey's Choice	$3.50
☐ MG45660-1	#59	Mallory Hates Boys (and Gym)	$3.50
☐ MG45662-8	#60	Mary Anne's Makeover	$3.50
☐ MG45663-6	#61	Jessi and the Awful Secret	$3.50
☐ MG45664-4	#62	Kristy and the Worst Kid Ever	$3.50
☐ MG45665-2	#63	Claudia's Freind Friend	$3.50
☐ MG45666-0	#64	Dawn's Family Feud	$3.50
☐ MG45667-9	#65	Stacey's Big Crush	$3.50
☐ MG47004-3	#66	Maid Mary Anne	$3.50
☐ MG47005-1	#67	Dawn's Big Move	$3.50
☐ MG47006-X	#68	Jessi and the Bad Baby-sitter	$3.50
☐ MG47007-8	#69	Get Well Soon, Mallory!	$3.50
☐ MG47008-6	#70	Stacey and the Cheerleaders	$3.50
☐ MG47009-4	#71	Claudia and the Perfect Boy	$3.99
☐ MG47010-8	#72	Dawn and the We ♥ Kids Club	$3.99
☐ MG47011-6	#73	Mary Anne and Miss Priss	$3.99
☐ MG47012-4	#74	Kristy and the Copycat	$3.99
☐ MG47013-2	#75	Jessi's Horrible Prank	$3.50
☐ MG47014-0	#76	Stacey's Lie	$3.50
☐ MG48221-1	#77	Dawn and Whitney, Friends Forever	$3.99
☐ MG48222-X	#78	Claudia and Crazy Peaches	$3.50
☐ MG48223-8	#79	Mary Anne Breaks the Rules	$3.50
☐ MG48224-6	#80	Mallory Pike, #1 Fan	$3.99
☐ MG48225-4	#81	Kristy and Mr. Mom	$3.50

More titles... ➤

The Baby-sitters Club titles continued...

☐ MG48226-2	#82	Jessi and the Troublemaker	$3.99
☐ MG48235-1	#83	Stacey vs. the BSC	$3.50
☐ MG48228-9	#84	Dawn and the School Spirit War	$3.50
☐ MG48236-X	#85	Claudi Kishi, Live from WSTO	$3.50
☐ MG48227-0	#86	Mary Anne and Camp BSC	$3.50
☐ MG48237-8	#87	Stacey and the Bad Girls	$3.50
☐ MG22872-2	#88	Farewell, Dawn	$3.50
☐ MG22873-0	#89	Kristy and the Dirty Diapers	$3.50
☐ MG22874-9	#90	Welcome to the BSC, Abby	$3.99
☐ MG22875-1	#91	Claudia and the First Thanksgiving	$3.50
☐ MG22876-5	#92	Mallory's Christmas Wish	$3.50
☐ MG22877-3	#93	Mary Anne and the Memory Garden	$3.99
☐ MG22878-1	#94	Stacey McGill, Super Sitter	$3.99
☐ MG22879-X	#95	Kristy + Bart = ?	$3.99
☐ MG22880-3	#96	Abby's Lucky Thirteen	$3.99
☐ MG22881-1	#97	Claudia and the World's Cutest Baby	$3.99
☐ MG22882-X	#98	Dawn and Too Many Sitters	$3.99
☐ MG69205-4	#99	Stacey's Broken Heart	$3.99
☐ MG69206-2	#100	Kristy's Worst Idea	$3.99
☐ MG69207-0	#101	Claudia Kishi, Middle School Dropout	$3.99
☐ MG69208-9	#102	Mary Anne and the Little Princess	$3.99
☐ MG69209-7	#103	Happy Holidays, Jessi	$3.99
☐ MG45575-3		Logan's Story Special Edition Readers' Request	$3.25
☐ MG47118-X		Logan Bruno, Boy Baby-sitter	
		Special Edition Readers' Request	$3.50
☐ MG47756-0		Shannon's Story Special Edition	$3.50
☐ MG47686-6		The Baby-sitters Club Guide to Baby-sitting	$3.25
☐ MG47314-X		The Baby-sitters Club Trivia and Puzzle Fun Book	$2.50
☐ MG48400-1		BSC Portrait Collection: Claudia's Book	$3.50
☐ MG22864-1		BSC Portrait Collection: Dawn's Book	$3.50
☐ MG69181-3		BSC Portrait Collection: Kristy's Book	$3.99
☐ MG22865-X		BSC Portrait Collection: Mary Anne's Book	$3.99
☐ MG48399-4		BSC Portrait Collection: Stacey's Book	$3.50
☐ MG92713-2		The Complete Guide to The Baby-sitters Club	$4.95
☐ MG47151-1		The Baby-sitters Club Chain Letter	$14.95
☐ MG48295-5		The Baby-sitters Club Secret Santa	$14.95
☐ MG45074-3		The Baby-sitters Club Notebook	$2.50
☐ MG44783-1		The Baby-sitters Club Postcard Book	$4.95

Available wherever you buy books...or use this order form.

Scholastic Inc., P.O. Box 7502, 2931 E. McCarty Street, Jefferson City, MO 65102

Please send me the books I have checked above. I am enclosing $_____
(please add $2.00 to cover shipping and handling). Send check or money order—
no cash or C.O.D.s please.

Name_____ Birthdate_____

Address _____

City_____ State/Zip _____

BSC5962

THE BABY-SITTERS CLUB®

by Ann M. Martin

Collect and read these exciting BSC Super Specials, Mysteries, and Super Mysteries along with your favorite Baby-sitters Club books!

BSC Super Specials

❏ BBK44240-6	Baby-sitters on Board! Super Special #1	$3.95
❏ BBK44239-2	Baby-sitters' Summer Vacation Super Special #2	$3.95
❏ BBK43973-1	Baby-sitters' Winter Vacation Super Special #3	$3.95
❏ BBK42493-9	Baby-sitters' Island Adventure Super Special #4	$3.95
❏ BBK43575-2	California Girls! Super Special #5	$3.95
❏ BBK43576-0	New York, New York! Super Special #6	$4.50
❏ BBK44963-X	Snowbound! Super Special #7	$3.95
❏ BBK44962-X	Baby-sitters at Shadow Lake Super Special #8	$3.95
❏ BBK45661-X	Starring The Baby-sitters Club! Super Special #9	$3.95
❏ BBK45674-1	Sea City, Here We Come! Super Special #10	$3.95
❏ BBK47015-9	The Baby-sitters Remember Super Special #11	$3.95
❏ BBK48308-0	Here Come the Bridesmaids! Super Special #12	$3.95
❏ BBK22883-8	Aloha, Baby-sitters! Super Special #13	$4.50

BSC Mysteries

❏ BAI44084-5	#1	Stacey and the Missing Ring	$3.50
❏ BAI44085-3	#2	Beware Dawn!	$3.50
❏ BAI44799-8	#3	Mallory and the Ghost Cat	$3.50
❏ BAI44800-5	#4	Kristy and the Missing Child	$3.50
❏ BAI44801-3	#5	Mary Anne and the Secret in the Attic	$3.50
❏ BAI44961-3	#6	The Mystery at Claudia's House	$3.50
❏ BAI44960-5	#7	Dawn and the Disappearing Dogs	$3.50
❏ BAI44959-1	#8	Jessi and the Jewel Thieves	$3.50
❏ BAI44958-3	#9	Kristy and the Haunted Mansion	$3.50
❏ BAI45696-2	#10	Stacey and the Mystery Money	$3.50

More titles ➡

The Baby-sitters Club books continued...

❑ BAI47049-3	#11 Claudia and the Mystery at the Museum	$3.50
❑ BAI47050-7	#12 Dawn and the Surfer Ghost	$3.50
❑ BAI47051-5	#13 Mary Anne and the Library Mystery	$3.50
❑ BAI47052-3	#14 Stacey and the Mystery at the Mall	$3.50
❑ BAI47053-1	#15 Kristy and the Vampires	$3.50
❑ BAI47054-X	#16 Claudia and the Clue in the Photograph	$3.99
❑ BAI48232-7	#17 Dawn and the Halloween Mystery	$3.50
❑ BAI48233-5	#18 Stacey and the Mystery at the Empty House	$3.50
❑ BAI48234-3	#19 Kristy and the Missing Fortune	$3.50
❑ BAI48309-9	#20 Mary Anne and the Zoo Mystery	$3.50
❑ BAI48310-2	#21 Claudia and the Recipe for Danger	$3.50
❑ BAI22866-8	#22 Stacey and the Haunted Masquerade	$3.50
❑ BAI22867-6	#23 Abby and the Secret Society	$3.99
❑ BAI22868-4	#24 Mary Anne and the Silent Witness	$3.99
❑ BAI22869-2	#25 Kristy and the Middle School Vandal	$3.99
❑ BAI22870-6	#26 Dawn Schafer, Undercover Baby-sitter	$3.99

BSC Super Mysteries

❑ BAI48311-0	The Baby-sitters' Haunted House Super Mystery #1	$3.99
❑ BAI22871-4	Baby-sitters Beware Super Mystery #2	$3.99
❑ BAI69180-5	Baby-sitters' Fright Night Super Mystery #3	$4.50

Available wherever you buy books...or use this order form.

Scholastic Inc., P.O. Box 7502, 2931 East McCarty Street, Jefferson City, MO 65102-7502

Please send me the books I have checked above. I am enclosing $ _____
(please add $2.00 to cover shipping and handling). Send check or money order
— no cash or C.O.D.s please.

Name_____Birthdate_____

Address _____

City_____State/Zip_____

Please allow four to six weeks for delivery. Offer good in the U.S. only. Sorry, mail orders are not
available to residents of Canada. Prices subject to change.

The New THE BABY-SITTERS CLUB® FAN CLUB

Only $8.95!
Plus $2.00 Postage and Handling

Sign up now for a year of great friendships and terrific memories!

★ **110-mm camera!**
Take photos of your pals!

★ **Mini-photo album**
Fill it with your best pics!

★ **Diary (with lock!)**
For your favorite memories...and secret thoughts!

★ **Stationery note cards and stickers**
Send letters to your far-away friends!

★ **Eight cool pencils**
With the signatures of different baby-sitters!

★ **Full-color BSC poster**

★ **Subscription to the official BSC newsletter***

★ **Special keepsake shipper**

Amazing stuff!

To get your fan club pack (in the U.S. and Canada only), just fill out the coupon or write the information on a 3" x 5" card and send it to us with your check or money order. U.S. residents: $8.95 plus $2.00 postage and handling to The New BSC FAN CLUB, Scholastic Inc. P.O. Box 7500, 2931 East McCarty Street, Jefferson City, MO 65102. Canadian residents: $13.95 plus $2.00 postage and handling to The New BSC FAN CLUB, Scholastic Canada, 123 Newkirk Road, Richmond Hill, Ontario, L4C3G5. Offer expires 9/30/97. Offer good for one year from date of receipt. Please allow 4-6 weeks for your introductory pack to arrive.

*First newsletter is sent after introductory pack. You will receive at least 4 newsletters during your one-year membership.